A Principal Murder

Geordan Richardson

Geordan Richardson

For the people who make me who I am today.

I love you Mam and Dad.

1

When you go to the principal's office, normally, it's never a good thing. But for Ryan Striker, it wasn't to get the proverbial 'slap on the wrist.' After all, Ryan hadn't been to school since he was fifteen and this was to be a more formal meeting with Mr. Mulrua, the principal of Callystown's local secondary school. Ryan had managed to get a ten-minute meeting with Mr. Mulrua at 9:15 am.

Ryan was nineteen years old, with an athletic build and confident persona. He walked briskly with an air of astute confidence, always upright and never with his hands in his pockets. His hair was short and brown. Ryan had kept the same hairstyle his whole life never bothering with fades or anything else that was trendy. Despite having bright green eyes; they were dark and older in tone like Ryan had seen things most people his age could only imagine in their nightmares. He dressed casually: in blue jeans and a slim fit t-shirt and jacket. Ryan was always more interested in looking functional over fashionable.

Callystown was a local town situated in Drogheda County Louth, close to Clogherhead village, famous for its sandy beaches attracting many tourists during the summer months. Those tourists never arrived before late April/early May, so it was easy for Ryan to walk to the school unbothered by crowds. Luckily he missed the rush hour of bored school-kids trudging in for another day of learning. Callystown was generally sunny and bright during the spring months. Yet dark clouds swam across the sky this morning. As Ryan approached the school gates, a sound of flustered footsteps followed him. He spun around and saw the sound to be coming from a very red-faced girl, about the same age as him wearing a uniform. She had long black hair and though she had a bright pleasant expression, Ryan noticed a hint of tears in her eyes, like she had been crying a few minutes earlier.

'Never seen someone in such a hurry to get to school,' Ryan said dryly.

The girl looked at him with a witty glint in her eyes and a playful arch to her brow, 'Really? Because I've never seen someone our age wear a military jacket in twenty-five-degree heat. You don't look like someone who's in the military.' A distinct accent coloured her words. Ryan immediately recognized it as Liverpudlian.

'That's because I'm not,' Ryan shot back. The two studied each other for a few seconds as they walked into the school.

'I'm Abigail'

'Ryan'

'So, what brings you to Callystown secondary school? You don't look like a student.' Abigail asked.

'I need to speak with the principal,'

'Mr. Mulrua?' Abigail looked surprised, 'How did you arrange a meeting? I've only seen him outside his office twice since I came here two years ago. He normally never sees people.'

'Perhaps he only sees people if it's important,' Ryan responded.

'Oh and yours is?' Abigail responded sarcastically. 'What do you need to see him about that's so important?'

'Information.'

They continued up to Mr. Mulrua's office, Abigail wanted to ask more but didn't think their conversation would come to anything. Ryan didn't seem like one for talking. Most boys Abigail knew in her year were quite loud, obnoxious, and loved to talk about themselves.

Ryan on the other hand seemed more reserved and private, but Abigail noticed a steely determination in his eyes, especially when he said the word 'information.' It was like he had been waiting and waiting to speak to Mr. Mulrua and wasn't going to let anything stand in his way. When they arrived at the office, the secretary told them Mr. Mulrua had arrived only fifteen minutes ago and was still getting set up in his office. She directed Ryan and Abigail to Mr. Mulrua's office down the hallway and to wait for him to call them. The office door was closed, the windows nearby were covered by blinds. You couldn't see into the office and this was no surprise. Many students went through their six years in school without ever seeing him. Mr. Mulrua was famously private and rarely stood in the limelight. Abigail knew he would never agree to hold meetings for fun. He was notoriously organised and stuck to a strict schedule. This only intrigued Abigail more as to why he had agreed to meet Ryan when he would only ever have an outsider in the school when absolutely necessary. It was only when the two sat down in the waiting area that Abigail noticed Ryan's puzzled face, probably as to why Abigail was still with him.

'I have to show him a note as to why I was late,' Abigail read the question he was about to ask.

'How pathetic is it someone your age has to show a "late note" to the principal?' Ryan scoffed. 'What a way to prepare teenagers for the real world.'

'You talk like you've seen it' Abigail replied with annoyance in her voice. 'You can't be that long out of school yourself.'

'I've been out long enough to know there's more to it than showing late notes to those in power,' Ryan snapped angrily. 'It's a world that eats you up, spits you out, and eats you again for the fun of it. It's where shitty things happen you can't stop and have no control over. You figure out fast enough, the world we live in is bitter, unforgiving and you have to fight for everything.'

Abigail was shocked at Ryan's response but couldn't process the information before the two heard a loud thud coming from inside Mr. Mulrua's office. The two glanced at each other and waited a few seconds.

Silence.

Ryan and Abigail slowly rose from their seats and cautiously approached the door. 'That sounded like Mr. Mulrua fell down or something,' Abigail whispered.

'I think we would be very lucky if that's all it was,' Ryan muttered. He tried to open the door, only to find it locked.

'Stand back,' Ryan told Abigail who obliged. Ryan took a few steps back, quickly moved forward, and kicked the door open. The door loudly hit the other side of the wall but the sight that greeted Ryan and Abigail was so shocking, the noise of the door didn't even register with them.

Mr. Mulrua was sitting dead in his chair, having been stabbed multiple times in the heart.

.

2

Mr. Mulrua was seated in his chair, leaned back with his hands dangling at his sides. His mouth was slightly open and his lifeless eyes were full of fear. His suit was covered in patches of blood making it was easy to see where he'd been stabbed. His chair was at his desk in the centre of the office, directly opposite the door.

Abigail's body went rigid. She began shaking and needed to hold on to the doorknob just to avoid falling. Her face paled as though she were about to faint. She had gone into shock, and could only mutter the words, "Oh my God." Her brain was unable to register what she was seeing. While it was obvious the scene was real, Abigail nonetheless tried to convince herself it wasn't. Only a bad dream or someone playing a cruel and grotesque joke.

Ryan on the other hand didn't flinch, his expression was impossible to read. He could have been angry, sad, or indifferent. He began studying the scene. The office was small and had no windows outside the one covered by blinds. There was a skeleton in his office that Mr. Mulrua used for demonstrations when he was teaching about the human body during science class. There was an open cupboard in the corner of the room containing shelves and a few books in it.

'Not really a hiding spot,' Ryan thought. There didn't seem to be a way into the office aside from the door which was locked from the inside, meaning one would assume no one but Mr. Mulrua could access the office as he had the only key. Of course, there were obscure ways of doing it, but they were quite difficult and often required multiple people. Ryan tried to process all these scenarios but was interrupted by a noise coming from the end of the hallway. He

immediately snapped out of his daze when he heard police sirens coming from outside.

'Abigail, we gotta go, now!' Ryan shouted. He began to help Abigail to her feet but she was still in shock from seeing Mr. Mulrua's body. Ryan knew he needed to do something more to alert her. He grabbed Abigail's shoulders, shook them a bit, and focused his eyes on hers. 'Abigail, listen to me, The Gardaí are here and they're going to see us standing in front of a dead principal with the door broken down. That alone will be enough to take us in for questioning. Your fingerprints will be on the doorknob and they can place us at the scene of the crime.'

Abigail's eyes slowly came more focused and began nodding her head slightly to show she understood. The Gardaí were coming closer and Ryan heard one of them shouting from down the hallway. He wasn't lying to Abigail when he said that the Gardaí would arrest them.

There was enough circumstantial evidence against them from Abigail's fingerprints on the doorknob and even the fact that Ryan had been scheduled to meet Mr. Mulrua. If they were caught Ryan would no doubt have to tell the police why he was meeting Mr. Mulrua, and under no circumstances could Ryan allow that to happen. He had come too far and worked too hard just to give up the information he had.

The school was a single building with one corridor going round in a circular motion. There were a few exit doors and a stairway to the second floor. Mr. Mulrua's office was on one side of the building with a stairway to the left and an exit straight ahead. Ryan and Abigail began sprinting down the other corridor away from the police. However, a group of four policemen turned the corner to block their path. Ryan and Abigail tried to turn back but another group of guards blocked the other way. Their last chance was the staircase. There was enough space between Ryan and the group of Guards to make the entrance to the stairs but just as Ryan turned the corner, another Guard raced down the stairs, blocking the path. They were surrounded.

'You're both under arrest for suspicion of murder!' one of the Guards shouted. 'Hands up!'

'Shit,' Abigail whispered, she still looked a bit dazed.

Ryan kept his face neutral, before slowly raising his hands. 'Sorry guys, I wish things could have been different.'

'Shut your mouth Striker! Save it for when you try to plead your innocence to the judge.'

'Oh, I wasn't talking about court,' Ryan replied.

The Guards looked confused. A small, cunning smile worked its way across Ryan's face.

'I was talking about this.'

3

In a flash, Ryan dropped one of his arms. A small ball fell out of his sleeve and hit the floor. Smoke exploded out which blurred the Guard's line of sight.

'Let's go!' Ryan shouted to Abigail.

The chances of them fighting through the two groups of guards to either side of them were slim. At that, there would no doubt be plenty more on the first floor. Taking out one Guard on the stairs though? That seemed a more feasible idea. Ryan and Abigail bolted up the stairs. The solitary guard on the stairs was confused by the smoke and Ryan took him out with a punch to the face and threw him over the side.

'Are you insane?!' Abigail roared. 'You could have killed him!'

'Maybe, but do you want to go check?' Ryan snapped back.

The other Guards began chasing them up the stairs. The staircase was only freshly cleaned that morning by caretakers making it quite slippery and necessary to cling on to the banister as they sprinted up. Arriving on the second floor, Ryan and Abigail were greeted by another group of three Guards this time equipped with batons and shields. Ryan nonetheless continued to race forward. Abigail followed.

'Alright genius, now what?!' Abigail shouted, panting for breath.

Ryan reached into his inside pocket, took out a gun, and with just three shots took out the guards, clearing the path. Abigail watched in horror, but couldn't get any words out before the other Guards from downstairs began gaining ground on them. The second floor also had one corridor designed in a circular motion. Ryan and Abigail were on a straight line of the corridor with a trapdoor leading to the roof of the school. Shouts from the Guards downstairs were getting louder.

'If we get to the roof, we might have a chance of getting away. The school corridors are flooded with guards.' Ryan said as they bolted towards the hatch at the end of the line of the corridor. The Guards behind them were still gaining ground though. Ryan and Abigail reached the hatch of the trapdoor. Ryan opened it and the two were able to climb onto the roof. Ryan then shut the hatch and slapped some nearby bricks on top to slow the Guards down. Dark ominous clouds continued to circle the sky and looked ready to explode at any minute. The roof was wide, flat, and most importantly, free of Gardaí.

'Do you have any idea what you're doing?!' Abigail screamed. 'You attacked policemen, killing some I might add, and now we're stuck on a two-story roof with no way of getting off, minutes away from going to jail. Did you think about this at all? Are you not scared of going to jail? What the hell are your parents going to say?'

Ryan's posture suddenly tensed which Abigail couldn't have missed. She knew she had touched a nerve. Ryan turned and stared at her without blinking. His eyes showed a flurry of emotions, anger, sadness, pain;… but not an ounce of fear.

'I do have an idea what I'm doing, I did think this through, I didn't kill those guards, I used a stun gun.' Ryan took out the gun and showed it to Abigail. Ryan wasn't lying. The gun was purely for stunning. As she looked at the gun Abigail's anger was replaced with fear. Her eyes began to tear up.

'I'm scared Ryan,' she sobbed.

Ryan's expression softened and a cheeky smile appeared on his face.

'Don't be, our rides about to arrive.'

At that moment, the two could hear music coming from a distance, Ryan ran to the edge of the roof and saw a pick-up truck speeding into the schoolyard.

'Right on time,' Ryan said with a smirk. 'We gotta jump.'

'Are you shitting me?' Abigail asked. 'This was your big plan? Jump?'

Ryan nodded at the hatch that was seconds away from being smashed open and shrugged.

Abigail looked stunned. Nerves started to build up and she began to shake.

'Trust me,' Ryan said calmly and held out his hand. Abigail took it.

'Ready?' Ryan asked. Abigail nodded her head. 'Count down with me.'

'Three,' Ryan started.

'Two,' Abigail continued.

'One,' Ryan's face was now excited.

'Jump!'

Ryan and Abigail made a run for the edge and jumped into the back of the truck. The driver had laid out a mattress to break their fall.

4

Chief Superintendent Jason Rafferty just wanted a normal day. It had been a difficult few months since he had been promoted to Chief Superintendent for the County Louth Garda Division. Rafferty and his wife had separated and his dad had died just a few weeks earlier. So the last thing he needed was a phone call at 9:40 am on a Monday morning to inform him that a principal in Drogheda had been murdered in his own office and that the main suspect had escaped. Rafferty was a well and able Garda having joined the force after completing his Leaving Cert and worked his way up the ranks until being promoted to Chief Superintendent. Rafferty has been living his childhood dream, upholding the law and pursuing social justice. Lately however, the workaholism, the separation, and lack of sleep had taken their toll. He was rarely seen without a cup of coffee, and his enthusiasm for his work was waning. It had gotten to the point that he was considering retirement in a few years. Upon arriving in Callystown, Rafferty saw the school surrounded by Garda cars and noticed it was flooded by Gardaí. The students had been sent home early due to the circumstances and a number of the younger ones were crying outside the school gates. Rafferty was informed of the incident by the District Officer for Drogheda Joseph Collins.

'Victim's name is Michael Mulrua, forty-nine years old, six foot one, arrived at his office at 8:30 am this morning. He was greeted by his secretary, who thought he was enthused as normal for the day ahead. At 9:15 am we received a letter saying that Mr. Mulrua was going to be in trouble this morning. I dispatched my officers to investigate. They discovered Mr. Mulrua dead in his chair at 9:32 am. We estimate he was killed sometime between 9:00 am and 9:30 am. His secretary informed us that two teenagers had arrived looking for Mr. Mulrua at 9:15 am. Those were the two people who attacked the Guards and escaped.' Collins recounted,

'Do we know who they are?' Rafferty asked.

'Yes Sir, Abigail Davies, eighteen, a sixth-year student here in Callystown school. The family is originally from Liverpool, England. According to the secretary, she had to show Mr. Mulrua a late note.'

'Pardon?' Rafferty replied with a confused look. 'Doesn't the secretary deal with that stuff?'

'Normally, yes,' Collins said. 'But Mr. Mulrua was fussy and wanted to process all that stuff himself. He felt his secretary had enough stuff to handle and wanted to ease the burden. He was a good man.' Collins looked shaken by the incident. 'What kind of bastard would do this?'

'One with a lot of anger. He was stabbed multiple times. This was a murder powered by emotion rather than stealth. I'd say whoever murdered Mr. Mulrua hated him severely.' Rafferty muttered. 'What about the second guy with Ms. Davies?'

'He's a little trickier. His name is Ryan Striker, nineteen years old. He's not local, and the secretary didn't recognise him. She said he told her he had a private meeting with Mr. Mulrua at 9:30 am. It's taking a little longer to get information on him.'

Rafferty laughed cynically, 'The cheeky little shit, private meeting? Now I really want to nail his ass. Did anyone else meet with the victim this morning?'

'According to the secretary, no one apart from Striker and Davies went to see the victim. Mr. Mulrua always went straight to his office, never to the staff room. None of the teachers saw him this morning. Apparently, he rarely agreed to meet with anyone, outside of processing late notes or if it was absolutely essential.'

'What about CCTV?'

'It's been very conveniently offline since this morning. We got nothing from it.'

Rafferty and Collins arrived at the crime scene. Rafferty observed the office and its furniture, and immediately noticed the lack of windows or exits.

'Is there any other way into the office apart from the door?' Rafferty asked.

'Not that we can tell, the door was broken in when my men arrived. They immediately pursued Striker and Davies but to no avail. Forensics picked up Davies' fingerprints on the jamb of the door. Any other D.N.A belonged to the victim. There's no evidence of another person in this office Sir.'

'Do Striker and Davies know each other?'

'We asked around and some of Davies' friends said they had never seen him before. Apparently, she isn't interested in having a boyfriend and she never mentioned a boy to her friends.' Collins paused for a moment. 'Sir, her parents have been worried sick. She is an only child and has no previous criminal convictions on her record. She is an exemplary student, and her teachers speak highly of her. She doesn't seem like someone who would be involved in something like this.'

Rafferty rubbed his face with both hands. 'From what I see, if there was no other way into the office, and no one else was in contact with the victim, we have to assume they are the guilty party. I want them found and brought in for questioning Officer Collins.'

'Sir why would two teenagers want to kill a principal?' Collins asked.

'I don't know, maybe he gave them one too many detentions!' shouted Rafferty. 'Look we have a dead principal with our only leads being two suspects who weren't even born when you joined the police force and yet still, they made a mockery of your men! Maybe if they had been caught and arrested earlier like they should have been it would be case closed! But that didn't happen did it, Officer?! Your men are an embarrassment to An Garda Siochana!' Rafferty's last statement brought all activity in the room to a complete stop. A few Guards looked on sheepishly. Collins continued to stare down Rafferty, he tried to keep a poker face, but it was easy to tell he wasn't going to let Rafferty's outburst slide.

'With the greatest respect, Sir,' Collins's voice was low but determined. 'You can say my men were slow to react, that they didn't handle the situation well, even that they were easily duped by Striker.' Collins paused for a moment. 'But never, ever insult my men like you just did there. They are all committed to helping solve this case and making amends for their errors this morning. If you take issue with them, I would like you to tell me now.' The two men continued to stare each other down. Finally, Rafferty spoke,

'Continue to look into background checks on Striker, I want to know everything about him.

What Collins didn't know was that Rafferty knew exactly who Ryan Striker was.

And it was the main reason why Rafferty was so concerned about the murder.

5

Ryan and Abigail rode on the truck for fifteen mins, long enough that the adrenaline of the chase had worn off and Abigail was starting to feel sick. The image of first seeing Mr. Mulrua dead in his chair was burned into her subconscious and the smell of death in the office still disgusted her. She was sweating all over and her hair badly needed a wash. It had already been a difficult morning after arguing with her parents about her life ambitions. To top it all off, she was riding in a truck with a strange guy who despite being no older than her, was able to escape a group of around thirty members of An Garda Siochana like he was pouring a cup of tea. She was tired, confused, and afraid. Ryan on the other hand just stared out into the distance. He seemed perfectly calm and was perfectly still, almost like he was meditating.

The truck pulled into a dilapidated neighbourhood. Many of the houses had their windows smashed and the streets were covered in empty beer cans and cigarette butts. The grass was overgrown and weeds were growing high at every curb. The walls looked like they hadn't been painted in years and besides graffiti was sprayed all over the walls. Many were messages of anger. Having been born into a reasonably wealthy family, the images in front of her made Abigail quite uncomfortable.

'Do you live here?' Abigail asked Ryan timidly.

'No,' Ryan responded. 'But I wouldn't go looking for someone who does. This is where we can hide from the police until we figure out our next move. It's off the grid. No one is going to come looking for us here.'

Abigail couldn't believe what she was hearing, 'Excuse me?! What the hell are we hiding from?' 'We haven't done anything wrong! Mr. Mulrua was dead when we opened that door.'

'The police would have arrested us right there on the spot if they found us.'

'How do you know that?'

'I know them.'

'From where?'

'A long time ago.'

'You don't talk much do you?'

Ryan didn't answer. The truck had pulled into a driveway at the end of a neighbourhood. Despite the house in front of them still looking dilapidated, Abigail noticed there was at least some love given. The grass was cut short, there was no litter to be found and the graffiti messages had been painted over. The house had a large garage to the left, which the truck stopped in front of, and a huge field behind it. It looked like it had once been used for farming before the grass got overgrown and uncared for.

'Is this your house?' Abigail asked Ryan.

'For the moment, yes, I share it with Miguel.'

'Who?'

'Our driver.'

At that moment the truck door opened, and a young guy hopped out. He had tanned skin suggesting he was Spanish or Portuguese. He was of average height, around five foot nine. He certainly wasn't overweight but was teetering on the edge of needing to lose a few pounds. He looked untidy, wearing dungarees and an old t-shirt with dirt all over his clothes. He wore glasses and had a kind face, though he didn't look happy to see Ryan.

'Damn it Striker, I'd appreciate it if you gave me the heads up you might be about to piss someone off so much you'd need my help to save you from a thirty-foot-high drop.' exclaimed the tanned guy.

'Wherever would the fun be in that?' Ryan replied hopping off the trailer.

'For me or you?'

'Both,'

'You think I have nothing better to do?'

'Obviously, if you came within ten minutes of calling you.'

The two looked at each other for a couple of seconds before the tanned guy started smiling to himself. 'It's good to see you Ryan.'

'Likewise Mr. Gutierrez.'

The two gave each other a warm embrace, with Abigail still standing behind stunned.

'Err, Ryan could you introduce me here?'

'Of course,' Ryan turned and faced her. 'This is my good mate, Miguel Gutierrez. He's a mechanic and computer geek. Miguel, this is Abigail.'

'I prefer computer-professional. Pleased to meet you Abigail.'

'She got messed up in the situation in Callystown.' Ryan explained.

'I heard about what happened. Ryan, what on earth were you doing in a secondary school?'

'I had to speak with the principal.'

'The one that was murdered? Crikey, you can certainly pick them.'

'Can someone please explain why we aren't going to the police?' Abigail asked irritably.

'I told you,' Ryan replied bluntly.

'No, you told me some garbage about them arresting us for the murder.'

'That's because we were the only two people present at the scene of the crime. I reckon Mulrua was dead less than an hour before we opened the door. That's enough for them to take us in. They'll want this wrapped up as quickly as possible.'

Abigail was starting to space out. Images of Mr. Mulrua were starting to pour into the forefront of her mind. She felt dizzy and her vision began to darken, and it caught the attention of Ryan and Miguel.

'I don't feel great guys.' Abigail muttered before falling into Ryan's arms who had raced over to catch her.

'Jesus, she looks dreadful.' Miguel observed with a concerned look on his face.

'She's in shock from earlier.' Ryan admitted. 'It was grotesque Miguel. Mulrua was stabbed countless times in the chest. Whoever did this was angry, very angry.'

'And now the police think that you're involved?'

'Any chance they have to nail me they're going to take it.'

Miguel put his hands on the back of his neck. 'You never answered why you wanted to meet Mr. Mulrua by the way.'

Ryan closed his eyes momentarily despite it triggering dark memories from his past. He was hoping Mr. Mulrua would have answers for him, but his death only raised more questions and there was only one word that Ryan was focused on right now. One person. And he said it to a stunned and worried Miguel.

'Jessica.'

6

Rafferty returned to his office at around 4 pm, poured a hot cup of coffee, and sat down to look at his computer. The drama was taking its toll on the already exhausted Superintendent who had arrived in Callystown after two and a half hours of sleep. There was a large bundle of paperwork on his desk that wasn't going to be done in the next hour before he usually went home. So, Rafferty took a large gulp of coffee and began going through it. Despite all the information and evidence in front of him, Rafferty had only one thing on his mind.

'Where does Striker fit into all of this?'

After all, Rafferty hadn't encountered Ryan since he disappeared six months ago. Since Rafferty and his colleagues had to admit they had been lying to Ryan about their research and efforts to fill their side of the deal the two parties had brokered. It was the start of Rafferty's life falling apart, so it wasn't a situation he wanted to revisit.

Looking into background checks on Michael Mulrua, everything Collins told him checked out. Michael was born and raised in Callystown. Apparently, he had suffered from anger issues when he was young but soon grew out of them before going to college. After graduating from secondary school he completed his Arts degree in Maths and Science before next completing his masters in teaching. He had taught in Callystown for thirty years before becoming principal nine years ago. He was hugely popular with staff and students and had a real love for teaching and education. There was no evidence of any financial problems or people taking issue with him. An all-around good guy with no enemies. The secretary had informed them that Michael had arrived as per normal, happy, enthused, and energetic.

'Lovely,' Rafferty thought, 'No obvious motive, a nearly impossible escape, how on earth did this happen?' It was clear no one could have entered the office as it was locked. However, Mr. Mulrua never locked his door as he didn't want to metaphorically and literally 'lock people out.' Yet the door was bashed in when police arrived on the scene. Only Striker and Davies were seen in that corridor at the time of the murder. So surely, they are the killers? But why would they do it? How do Striker and Davies even know each other?

These questions were going back and forth in Rafferty's head and the cup of coffee was not helping him stay awake. He was also starting to feel regret about his outburst at Officer Collins. The murder at Callystown was a disaster for the local community and local police. Certainly, Collins and his crew should have reacted better to Ryan's escape, but he had no right to speak to Collins as he did. In truth, he was feeling regret about a lot of things. His life had peaked after becoming Chief Superintendent, but everything went wrong afterward. He had distanced himself from his closest friends in An Garda Siochana after the incident with Ryan. Followed directly by a mental and physical slump during the period of his father's death and separation from his wife.

His dad had taken a massive heart attack while playing golf and Rafferty had spent weeks praying by his side, hoping for a miracle, yet…, no such luck. Rafferty and his wife had been having problems with having a baby over the last few years, and it had become the crux of arguments, bitterness, and blame among both parties. They had split up properly three months ago and Rafferty missed her bitterly. He suffered stomach pains every day and hated waking up alone every morning.

Rafferty was about to tell himself to snap out of it when one of his younger officers came into his office with some news.

'Sorry for disturbing you Superintendent Rafferty, but we think we know where Striker is hiding.'

7

The house where Ryan and Miguel lived had a front porch with a couch that allowed you to look out onto the street. At night-time, you could regularly hear the sound of fireworks going off in the distance, the noise of drunken residents singing, or worst of all, fights breaking out and ambulances being called.

Ryan stood leaning out on the front of the porch staring into the darkness. He had told Miguel his side of what happened at Callystown. The discovery of Mulrua's body, Ryan's analysis of the crime scene, and their escape. Now he stood in silence pondering his next move while Miguel was inside looking after Abigail who was passed out on the couch. Miguel then emerged with a warm cup of coffee in his hand. He thought about offering Ryan one but thought it unlikely Ryan would want one in his current mindset.

'It's all over the local news Ryan,' Miguel told him. 'It's not going to be long before they find us here.'

'Then we'll move again,' Ryan responded.

'What exactly is the end goal here Ryan?' Miguel asked irritably. 'You've spent weeks trying to dig into Jessica's disappearance and gotten nowhere. You've spent months hiding here after what happened with you and the police. Now you're the chief suspect in the murder case of a respected local principal and in danger of being arrested. What exactly are you going to do?'

Ryan turned and faced him. 'I'm going to keep looking, Miguel. I'm going to dig into Mulrua's background and especially the last few days before his death. See if I find anything suspicious.'

'What on earth do you think you're going to find? What's going on Ryan?'

'Mulrua told me he knew about what happened to Jessica.'

This news hit Miguel like a ton of bricks. 'What?! When? How?'

'Yesterday, he sent me this email,' Ryan whipped out his phone and showed Miguel.

Ryan,

Throughout my whole life, I've made mistakes, I've been wrong, arrogant, cowardly, and insecure many times. Despite being in my mature years, I still make these same kinds of errors in judgment I should have told you sooner, but for my foolishness and fear, I did not. Now I want to make amends.

I know what happened to your dear Jessica. And I want to tell you personally why it has taken me this long for the truth to come out. Come to the school tomorrow and meet me in my office at 9:15 am.

I hope you will forgive me.

Kind Regards

Michael Mulrua

Miguel read it three times and still couldn't believe what he was reading. 'He knew where she is?'

'And what happened.' Ryan almost had a giddy look on his face. 'You think I'm going to give up the chase now?'

'Mulrua's suggesting he knew for ages, that he's bottled up lots of things over the years, even holding himself somewhat responsible.'

'And within twenty-four hours of sending the email, he's dead.'

The two men looked at each other with both fear and concern.

'Something sinister is going on,' Miguel murmured. 'You're not going to tell the police this are you?'

Ryan turned away and looked out into the darkness. 'Over my dead body.'

Miguel sighed. 'You can certainly hold a grudge, can't you?'

Ryan spun around. 'No, I just don't tolerate liars, or those who are willing to screw you over just to suit themselves and exploit you!' he snapped back.

Miguel was slightly taken aback by Ryan's outburst but knew it was a sensitive topic.

'Not all policemen are bad Ryan, and this could help clear your name.'

'Do you think I care about going to jail? Do you think I care if people think I killed Mulrua? All I'm concerned about is getting Jessica back, and I certainly don't need police to help me do so.'

'Who is Jessica?'

Ryan and Miguel jumped in surprise to see Abigail standing in the doorway.

'You're better!' Miguel exclaimed.

'How much of that did you hear?' Ryan asked in fury.

'Oh, nothing much, just something about an email from Mr. Mulrua, your grudge against An Garda Siochana and a mysterious Jessica. I'm sure you can fill in the rest.'

'Like hell, I will.' Ryan replied with gritted teeth.

'Yeah, I thought you would say that. You don't seem like one who would open up. Well, I guess I'd better be off then.'

'What, now?! At night?' Miguel asked with a worried look.

'You're going nowhere.' Ryan warned.

'Oh, shut up Striker, Do you think I'm going to hang around here while the police come chasing us down? I did nothing wrong and I'm not hibernating from the world in this dump.'

Ryan weighed up his options. If Abigail left, she would go home to worried parents and police who would want her to talk. She seemed to already know too much, and Ryan couldn't have his information fall into the police's hands. However, he didn't want to tell anyone else about Jessica. And he certainly didn't trust Abigail with knowing. Not yet at least.

'If you want me to stay, tell me what's going on.'

'Err... guys do you hear that?' Miguel asked cautiously.

The sounds of singing and fireworks had died out and were replaced by police sirens.

'Damn,' Ryan muttered. 'They found us.'

8

Multiple Garda cars came speeding up the road towards the house. The sound of the engine roaring managed to drown out the noise of the sirens.

'Everyone get into the truck!' Ryan shouted. The three sprinted into the truck where it had been parked outside the garage. Ryan took the driver's seat while Miguel and Abigail jumped into the back.

'Careful with her Ryan, I only just finished fixing the engine.' Miguel sighed.

'Try not to kill us jackass.' Abigail muttered.

Ryan started the truck and accelerated out of the garden into the overgrown field behind the house. 'We can lose them in the field. The grass is too long for Garda cars to drive through.'

'Oh, and this rust bucket won't have an issue?' Abigail sneered.

'You underestimate the craft of Spanish mechanics,' Ryan replied. 'Miguel, did you get that... "accessory" sorted?'

'Button beside the gearstick.' Miguel cockily answered.

Ryan pressed the button and suddenly the sound of blades screeching could be heard. Two holes had opened at the front of the truck and two steel razor blades emerged and were cutting away the grass that had probably been left for years without being touched. They sliced through like a hot knife through butter and meant the truck could speed through the field.

'Impressive,' Ryan remarked.

'Hasn't that just left a clear path for the police?' Abigail asked.

Ryan and Miguel looked behind them and sure enough, the path was obvious where they had gone and clear from where the blades had sliced through. The Garda cars were gaining on them.

Fast.

'Miguel, do you have any tools in the back of the truck?' Ryan asked.

Miguel began rummaging at his feet. 'Not much to work with, a few stun guns.'

'Any loaded ones?' Ryan probed.

Abigail looked at him in shock. 'You're not actually going to attempt this?'

'Found one.' Miguel handed it over to Ryan.

'Miguel take the wheel.' Ryan said before opening the truck door and leaning out with the gun in his hand. He started firing off shots at the tires and hit two in the first couple of rounds. The car whose tires he hit skidded to the side before stopping. Ryan came back in to reload much to Abigail's dismay.

'How do you think this is going to pan out? Do you think they'll just forget about the case and move on? They will keep coming back until they put you under arrest and you are only delaying the inevitable.'

'They can't arrest me if I can prove I'm innocent.' Ryan shot back while reloading. He hopped out again and fired more shots. This time hitting two more tires and sending their cars offroad.

'That's the last of the bullets Ryan.' Miguel informed him as Ryan came back in. He had gotten rid of three Garda cars but there were still plenty more tailing them.

'Miguel, can this go any faster?' Ryan asked.

'It's an old 07 truck Ryan, I'm amazed it's moving at all.' Miguel responded stressed. 'Listen we aren't going to outrun them, there are ten squad cars behind, and they're all going faster than us. Just call it quits.'

'I never had you down as a defeatist,' Ryan responded with a disappointed look on his face.

'He's being realistic you idiot!' Abigail screamed back. 'Cut the alpha male crap, swallow your pride, and stop the car! Every second we spend in here pisses them off even more.'

Ryan paused for a few seconds. 'Miguel, remember you were talking about installing a turbo boost to the truck?'

A look of horror appeared on Miguel's face. 'Ryan, if you're thinking what I think you're thinking,'

'Yes or no Miguel?'

Miguel looked nervous and almost began shaking, before slowly nodding his head.

'Yes.' He answered. 'But Ryan I've done no tests, no preparation, we're working with a brand-new engine. The likeliest outcome is that the engine explodes.'

Now it was Abigail's turn to look scared.

'Please... no.'

'Fasten your seatbelts guys.' Ryan had a look of pure fire in his eyes.

Ryan flicked open a switch beside his seat and hit it. It sounded like something was injected, but the engine didn't respond.

Miguel and Abigail exchanged worried looks.

In a split second, the car shot forward. They went from eighty to two-hundred kilometres per hour. The sheer force and power of the car knocked Ryan, Abigail, and Miguel backward. They were successful in getting away from the police, but the engine was overheating. Smoke started to appear in front of them. Abigail started praying while Miguel closed his eyes.

Ryan on the other hand kept his hands on the wheel and faced forward.

They came to the end of the field and Ryan had to turn sharply to stay on the road and on course. The boost was wearing off and the truck started to slow down. Ryan looked behind him and there were no Garda cars to be seen.

'Looks like the turbo works, Miguel,' Ryan remarked with a smirk.

Miguel gave a sarcastic thumbs up but didn't look pleased that Ryan ignored his warnings. Abigail on the other hand looked like she was ready to kill Ryan.

'You just don't care, do you?' she exclaimed.

'Excuse me?' Ryan asked.

'Look at what you've done in the last fifteen minutes, you have shot at police cars, resisted arrest, almost blown the engine. Do you understand how close you just came to killing us?'

'I didn't, did I?'

Miguel put his hand on his forehead in disappointment. He too was angry with Ryan's actions but had a better understanding of why Ryan was the way he was.

Abigail was still seething. 'Right either you're totally psychotic and unemotional or just reckless, self-centred, and don't care for the wellbeing of others. So Striker, which one is it?'

Ryan turned his head slightly towards the back, 'I do care about others.' Miguel picked up on a tinge of sadness in his voice. Abigail didn't unfortunately.

'Oh yes, the wonderful Jessica I still know sod all about. C'mon, who is she? Some pretty girlfriend who copped on what a total jerk you are and left you for someone more charming and charismatic?'

Abigail knew she had hit a nerve instantly. She could feel Miguel wincing beside her and Ryan seemingly gripped the steering wheel tightly.

'Why did you stay, Abigail?' Ryan asked after a few moments.

Abigail was taken aback by the change in topic. 'What...how is that relevant?'

'You could have left as soon as you woke back at the house, yet you stayed. You could have ran as soon as the Guards arrived and not jumped in the truck, yet you came. And now… you could jump out of the truck now and go to your old life. We're almost out of gas and I need to keep moving so I wouldn't come back to get you. So, if you want to leave now Abigail... be my guest.'

Both Ryan and Miguel looked at Abigail with anticipation. Abigail looked stunned like she had been caught stealing at the local supermarket or she had been found guilty in court.

A few minutes passed. Abigail said nothing.

'Thought so,' Ryan replied. 'So, now that you're going to stay there's only one thing you should know about me.' He looked her in the eyes. 'I am the way I am because I have to be. I've learned that I can trust no one, but most importantly of all, never think for a second that I don't care.'

Ryan turned back to face the road. Abigail sat there in silence too shocked to speak. Miguel looked out the window trying to distract himself until Ryan asked, 'Miguel where is the nearest hotel?' They had been driving in silence for half an hour.

'I think Glenside is only fifteen minutes away.'

'Right, that's where we're stopping then.' Ryan replied.

9

Superintendent Rafferty hadn't any expectations of getting much sleep tonight but certainly could've done without getting a call at 11 pm to say that three Garda cars had been sent off-road by bullets in their tires. So he poured himself a hot cup of coffee and drove out to the scene of the incident where he was again greeted by Joseph Collins.

'Please, tell me you have good news in the middle of all this,' an exhausted Rafferty pleaded.

'Unfortunately not Sir', Collins replied. 'My men discovered where Striker was and sent a team to bring him in. However, he escaped in a truck and shot the tires of some of the cars to stop them from following.'

'Shit,' Rafferty muttered under his breath. 'What about Davies?'

'She was seen getting into the truck along with Striker and another male. We've identified him as Miguel Gutierrez. Still looking for more information on him.'

Rafferty nodded. 'Thank you, Joseph.'

'There's another development, Sir,'

'What's that?'

'Abigail Davies's parents are here. They want to know if-'

'Superintendent Rafferty!' a distressed woman came rushing over to them. Where is my daughter?!' 'What's going on?'

'Madam, unfortunately there is very little we can tell you at this time.' Rafferty tried to reply.

'Is she in danger?'

Rafferty had to pause for a moment. 'No, I don't believe she is.' Collins shot him a puzzled glance.

'But isn't she with the chief suspect of a murder case?' Mrs. Davies shouted at him.

'We believe she is with a person of interest' Rafferty replied holding his nerve. 'Mr. Striker is just another party we would like to speak to. I don't suspect him as much as the media suggest. I don't believe Abigail is in danger with him, or Mr. Gutierrez.'

'Is it true he blew up Garda cars?'

'As I said Mrs. Davies there is very little I can divulge-'

'ARE YOU GOING TO GET MY DAUGHTER BACK?' Mrs. Davies screamed, starting to get hysterical.

'Yes, Yes I can promise you that,' Rafferty replied with confidence.

Two officers then came over and escorted Mrs. Davies away, leaving Rafferty and Collins alone.

'Could you fill me in, Sir?' Collins asked with annoyance. 'I was under the impression Striker WAS our one and only suspect.'

Rafferty turned and faced him.

'I haven't been overly truthful with you, Joseph. But no, I don't believe Striker is the killer.'

Collins couldn't believe what he was hearing. 'So, why the hell are we busting our balls trying to catch him? And why is he not turning himself in? He's all over the news. He took out police cars just to escape and assaulted multiple Guards in Callystown! He's in shit even if he is innocent of murder.'

Rafferty rubbed his eyes before answering. 'He's not concerned about being found innocent or guilty for the crime. He's concerned about being arrested.'

Collins was even more confused. 'Sir, I don't follow.'

'Just because he isn't the killer, doesn't mean he has nothing to do with the case. Him arranging a meeting with Mr. Mulrua hours before he's found dead is no coincidence.'

'Well, why would he have been in contact?'

'There's only one reason I can think of.' Rafferty replied gravely. 'And I think it's why he's on the run. It's the same reason he ran from me all those years ago.'

Poor Collins was losing the will to live.

'Sir you're going to have to fill me in.'

Rafferty had a sad smile on his face. 'Let me tell you the story of Ryan Striker....'

10

Ryan, Miguel, and Abigail arrived at Glenside that night, got checked in, and spent much of the night in the hotel room. Ryan went down to the pool late at night while Miguel sat in the room looking at his computer. Abigail sat on her bed in silence, thinking about what Ryan had said earlier.

'Why did you stay?'

The day had been such a blur that Abigail hadn't even thought about it. There was nothing really that Ryan or Miguel could have done to stop her, so why didn't she go? In the back of her mind, she knew why, but it was only starting to register with her. It all came back to the argument she had with her parents that morning before going to school. Above all else, however, she felt horrible about how she behaved in the truck. Yes, she was stressed and afraid, but also rude and obnoxious. No wonder Ryan wasn't telling her anything about who Jessica was. Why would he?

'You're awfully quiet there Scouse,' Miguel mused as he continued typing.

She was deep in thought and had to snap out to hear what Miguel was saying. 'Is that my new nickname?' she responded sarcastically with a small smile.

'Well, it looks like you're part of the team now, so you gotta have a nickname. I've always liked Scousers, always fun, optimistic, glass half full sort of guys.'

'Not really fitting in with me so far.' Abigail answered. 'I've been a total bitch.'

Miguel started laughing. 'Don't be too hard on yourself. This has been a really difficult day for you, a world away from your normal life.'

'I just feel awful about the way I acted.'

'Well... true, you didn't give your best impression. But, Ryan's not the best when it comes to giving black and white answers to what you were asking. And I don't know anyone else as distrustful of people.' Miguel paused for a moment. 'But he's also the most helpful, loyal, and reliable friend I could've asked for.'

'You two are obviously close?'

'We lived together throughout the pandemic, I got to know him really well, he got to know me really well. We were always there to help each other out.'

'How did the pandemic affect you, Miguel?' Abigail asked curiously.

'You mean how did it affect my stomach!' Miguel laughed. 'No seriously, those first few weeks? KitKats in the evening and unlimited time to watch Netflix? Not a good combination.'

Abigail chuckled to herself. 'C'mon you're not that bad.'

'I have started to get back into shape, that's the good thing about living with Ryan. He's always in the gym, running, swimming, boxing, and eating healthily. He does keep you on your toes.'

Abigail nodded in agreement.

'I did use it as a chance to learn new hobbies, I worked as a freelancer in the gig economy and made good money doing one-off gigs like setting up websites, designing business logos. It paid the bills, and left enough time to work on other projects.'

'Like razor blades in trucks?' Abigail smirked.

'Amongst other things!' Miguel laughed.

Abigail had had enough of feeling sorry for herself. 'Right I'm going to see Ryan and say sorry. Is he still down at the pool?' she asked as she walked to the door. Ryan had gone for a swim as soon as they arrived.

'Should be... oh and Scouse?'

Abigail turned and looked at Miguel.

'Don't push him for answers, he'll tell you in his own time,' Miguel whispered with a wink.

Abigail smiled and went down to the pool, which was situated on the ground floor. The reception area was very quiet as Abigail walked past and there was no one in the pool area except Ryan himself. He was busy doing laps of a two-hundred metre pool at a pretty serious speed, which Abigail took note of. Despite the events of the day, Ryan didn't seem fatigued at all, while Abigail could hardly stand on her own two feet.

'Ryan!' she shouted as she entered the pool area.

Ryan looked up, paused for a few seconds, and swam over to where Abigail was sitting on the pool edge and sat beside her. He wasn't an overly big guy, but very lean and fit with good muscle definition. 'I was just finished, I think it was forty laps in total of that pool.'

Abigail was surprised to hear that. 'Are you not exhausted from earlier on?'

'Tiredness is always in the head, the mind always fails before the body.' Ryan answered emphatically. 'Plus, it helps me sleep.'

'I should try it sometime,' Abigail murmured.

'So, what's up?' Ryan asked.

Abigail took a deep breath. 'I'm sorry for the way I spoke to you earlier.'

Ryan looked up with an amused look on his face.

Abigail continued, 'I was still wound up about seeing Mr. Mulrua and being in the middle of a murder investigation. I just snapped. I didn't know what was going on.'

'That's because I didn't tell you,' Ryan replied.

Abigail thought about what Miguel said up in the room but wanted to push her luck. 'Can you tell me now?'

Ryan had a smile on his face. 'It seems we both have questions that need answering. I'll answer yours if you answer mine.'

Abigail looked surprised. 'Ok... what do you want to ask?'

'The same one I asked you earlier. Why didn't you leave?'

The question hit Abigail hard, but at least she had an answer now.

'Because I didn't want to.'

11

Ryan was listening attentively. 'I noticed your eyes were teary this morning when we first met. You looked upset about something.'

'I argued with my parents this morning, about college choices.'

'Oh?'

Over the past few years, as I've gotten older, I've realised that so many people follow the same path in life. Go to school, go to college with a student job, graduate without a penny to your name because you spent all your money on partying and your fees, get a job, work forty hours a week, get taxed loads, have barely enough time or money left outside of your bills, holiday for two weeks, retire, die.'

Ryan nodded as if he was agreeing.

'This morning my parents were asking me where I wanted to go and what I wanted to do. And we had a huge argument because I said I didn't know.'

Ryan's eyes widened. 'You have no idea at all?'

Abigail sighed. 'I know I want to do something… exciting. Something that isn't normal or specialised. Something that I'll look back on when I'm on my deathbed and think, wow, what a great ride.' She looked up at the ceiling and pondered her thoughts.

'And your parents don't want that?' Ryan guessed.

'Nope, they want me to do something more reliable and safe, like a teacher or accountant. And I was afraid of going on the same path that so many other people do in life. Work at something they don't really care about, but do it anyway because it's safe, reliable, and pays the bills.'

Ryan nodded again.

'So, when I met you this morning and after everything that happened, while I was scared and pissed off with you, I was doing something exciting and unique. It was like two different sides of me were fighting each other in the truck. One saying, 'you're in danger, get out.' The other saying, 'isn't this what you wanted?'

'And what do you think now?'

Abigail looked at her reflection in the pool. 'I don't know. I don't have an exciting life Ryan, I have never had an exciting life. Throughout COVID my family was very strict about what I could do. I couldn't go to parties, discos, or bars unless the disease rates were very, very low. I was stuck inside with them for most of the pandemic. I know this sounds horrible to say... but, I'm sick of them. I just...don't know what I want.'

Ryan was taking this all in and thought for a moment before speaking again. 'She wasn't my girlfriend by the way.'

Abigail shot him a confused glance. 'Sorry?'

'You asked me if Jessica was my girlfriend earlier, she wasn't.'

'Then who was she?'

Ryan closed his eyes momentarily, took a deep breath, and answered.

'My sister.'

12

6 years earlier- December 18th, 2018

'Alright Strikers, it's time for our annual Christmas Monopoly game session!' Mr. Striker shouted up the stairs at his three children Jake, Ryan, and Jessica. Jake was fourteen, Ryan was twelve, and Jessica was ten. Every Christmas exactly a week before the big day, the Striker family would spend the afternoon playing Monopoly. Whoever had the most money after four hours would get to pick the Christmas movie for that night.

'Are you ready to get destroyed, little brother?' Jake sneered as they sprinted down the stairs.

'I'm only ever ready to win Jakey,' young Ryan replied cheekily.

'I just want to buy one of the red pieces,' exclaimed an innocent Jessica.

'You mean a hotel?' Jake asked.

'Yeah, but one with a pool, room service, a nicely decorated reception, one where a princess would stay.' Jessica closed her eyes imagining the princess lying on her bed ordering room service.

Jake and Ryan looked at each other and started roaring laughing. As the three kids arrived in the kitchen, they saw Mrs. Striker had the board set out already and with the correct starting budgets out on the table.

'Ok, now everyone starts with one-thousand euro as we agreed. No one snake extra money from the box. Jake honey, I'm looking at you.' Mrs. Striker looked at her eldest son with a firm but smiley look.

'I promise,' Jake replied before taking a peek at where the five-hundred notes were in the box.

The family played for the next four hours. When there were five minutes left to play, Ryan and

Jake were one-hundred euros apart with Jake leading.

'Looks like we're watching 'Die Hard' tonight lad,' Jake preached as Ryan sat looking carefully at the board.

'Can't eat the Christmas turkey before it's cooked, Jake.' Ryan replied. 'You'll get sick.'

A couple of minutes passed and it was Jake's throw with twenty seconds left. He took his time shaking.

'You're going to have to throw that before the timer runs out Jakey,' Ryan teased.

Jake rolled for the final time and rolled a five. He looked at Ryan as he moved. 'Better luck next time little brother.' Jake smiled as he moved on to the final piece while continuing to stare at Ryan.

Ryan started to smile while maintaining eye contact, then chuckle, before bursting out laughing along with the rest of the Strikers, much to Jake's confusion. He looked down at the board to see that he had landed on O'Connell Street, where Ryan had a hotel.

'GOD DAMN IT!!!' Jake shouted as the rest of the family continued laughing.

'Looks like we're not watching Die Hard then,' smiled Ryan.

'Never liked Monopoly anyway,' muttered Jake. 'Always said it was overrated.'

'I better start doing dinner,' Mrs. Striker exclaimed rising from the table and looking at the clock. 'I need someone to go to the shop and get mince. Ryan could you?'

'Yeah, no hassle' Ryan answered.

'I'm coming!' shouted little Jessica running for her red elf hat.

Ryan and Jessica left the house and walked the twenty minutes towards their local SuperValu. Snow was starting to fall and Christmas lights were all over bars and restaurants as they walked through town.

'I'm so happy Dad got Christmas off this year,' Jessica exclaimed as they walked.

Mr. Striker was a policeman and generally always had to work over Christmas, but thanks to pulling a few strings he managed to get two full weeks off this one.

'I know, this year there's no need to worry about trying to arrange activities around his shifts. We can pick and choose as we please.'

'Jake didn't look too happy about losing Monopoly,' Jessica smirked.

'That's because he always gets ahead of himself. He probably would've won if he was more focused towards the end instead of gloating,' Ryan was smiling to himself. 'But that's his prerogative, I suppose.'

'He's just jealous,' Jessica taunted. 'I have never seen you get cocky.'

'I guess I've got more control.'

They went into SuperValu, got their mince, and went up to the checkout. The place was quite busy the week before Christmas but Ryan and Jessica were still able to hear the radio.

'Anyone driving tonight in Dundalk is advised to use the motorway as there is heavy traffic build-up in the town centre due to a fire in the Hoey's Lane residential estate'

Ryan and Jessica shot a feared glance at each other. 'That's our estate!' Ryan shouted. They sprinted out of the SuperValu and back home. What they saw shocked them to the core. Jessica collapsed to her knees and started crying. Ryan just stared with an empty feeling in his eyes.

Their house was on fire.

13

Ryan blinked as if the memories were causing him pain, even remembering them. 'I tried running in to save them,' he whispered. 'I tried shouting their names, but there was no response. The house was falling apart. I had to be pulled out by firemen.'

Abigail was horrified by Ryan's story. 'Did they find out what caused it?'

Ryan shook his head looking at the floor. 'It went down as a 'faulty wiring incident,' which is total bullshit. The police never bothered to investigate past a certain point because there was little to no evidence left. They never found my parent's remains.'

Abigail wasn't expecting that. 'But didn't they die in the fire?'

Ryan shrugged his shoulders. 'No evidence of them ever being in the fire or in the house. But appeals went out for them after the fire, search parties were arranged but never turned up anything. They just vanished. Police gave up after a week.'

Abigail felt terrible for Ryan, but curiosity was taking over and she was wondering about a few more things. 'Is that why you don't want to hand yourself over to them now? Because you feel they didn't do your family justice?'

'Yes. And no, but in a much worse way.'

14

'I remember a young kid walking into my office, looking into his eyes and seeing so many emotions. Anger, fear, heartache but above all else, determination, and resolve.' Rafferty told his story to a curious Collins. 'He and his sister had nowhere to go, no aunts, uncles, grandparents. Both Mr. and Mrs. Striker were only children.'

'So, where did Striker go?' Collins asked.

'Well that was the first surprise, I received a call from the District Officer for Drogheda, my old friend Andrew Keaton, who told me that he was Striker's godfather. He had done police training with Ryan's dad, Richard.'

'So, he took them in?'

'Straight away. All seemed sorted until myself and Andrew made a bit of an error of judgment.'

Collins was listening.

'Crime amongst young people had been on a steady rise. There were huge increases in drug use, severe bullying, and suicide amongst teenagers. Unfortunately, the local police force wasn't large enough to deal with problems among young people. So, we needed someone with a young person's mind, someone who would have a more practical skillset to investigate said issues.'

'Ryan Striker.' Collins deduced

'He had everything needed to be a policeman. I saw all the tell-tale signs. Bravery, calmness under pressure, athletic ability, resourcefulness, and even a detective's mind. He was the perfect candidate. But at first, he was reluctant. He was still getting over what happened to his parents. So myself and Andrew as the two District Officers for Louth at the time agreed that in return for Striker's services in cleaning up teenage crime, we would keep the case file of the fire open, and keep it open until we figured out what happened. We also offered him a salary of fifteen-thousand euros a year, and full police training so he would be able to deal with all the aspects of being a Guard. Finally, a private tutor so he could continue his academic studies up until Leaving Cert.'

'The Chief Superintendent agreed to all this?'

'He was apprehensive but knew something had to be done about the rising wave of teenage crime. So he agreed on the basis that it was kept fairly hush-hush.'

'Did the plan work?'

'For a few years, yes, Ryan broke up several little petty gangs who were drug dealing and setting off fireworks into local supermarkets. He rarely had to deal with anyone much older than himself and always did it silently. The crime rates dropped, we were getting praise from our Superintendent and all was good. Ryan even seemed to be enjoying his job. I think he felt proud doing what his dad did.'

'But something did go wrong.'

'Andrew and I had tried to keep our side of the deal, but there was nothing we could find that explained how the Striker fire started. No eyewitnesses, no physical evidence, no CCTV, nothing We were devoting too many resources and staff to the case and the Superintendent started to get impatient. He wanted the case file shut and to move on to other cases.'

'But you promised Striker the file would stay open.'

'Eventually, we were forced to close the file. Andrew wanted to tell Ryan that it was case closed but I insisted we tell him nothing. He was doing so well and we couldn't afford to lose him. Andrew and I argued for ages about it, but Andrew eventually saw my line of thinking. Unfortunately, Striker discovered for himself.'

Collins's eyes widened. 'How?'

'He was getting antsy that we hadn't updated him on the case, so he went snooping into the active case files and saw that the Striker fire one had been shut.'

Collins winced. 'Then what?'

'He flipped out, called me every name under the sun, said he would never work for An Garda Siochana again as long as I was still alive.'

'Jesus that must've been hard to take,'

'It was even harder for Andrew. Striker was angry at me, but felt furious that his godfather would use him like that. He ran away a few nights later with Jessica, took all belongings, and wasn't seen or heard from again. That was three years ago.'

'How did Keaton take it?'

'Poor Andy was distraught. He felt he had let Richard down and betrayed his trust. He left the force a few weeks later, haven't heard from him since.' Rafferty paused for a moment, almost with tears in his eyes thinking back to the final phone call he had with his colleague and friend. 'It was one of my biggest regrets in all my time working for the Guards.'

'You stayed though, Sir,' Collins tried to comfort him. 'You didn't walk away.'

'Back then Collins, I was a workaholic, I worked sixty hours a week, working my way up the ranks to where I am today. I was successful, but it totally strained my relationship with my wife. Ended up with us getting divorced.' Rafferty had always looked and wondered how things may have been different if he had chosen a different path. 'Needless to say, teenage crime spiked again, and the pandemic only exacerbated the problem.'

'So why do you think Striker has shown his face again?'

'Ryan's sole motivation when he worked for us was providing for Jessica and deducing what happened to the rest of his family. My guess? That's what's motivating him now.'

15

Abigail couldn't believe Ryan's story of his time as a private contractor for An Garda Siochana. 'So what happened after you left with Jessica?'

Ryan was reliving some of his most hateful memories but was relieved to revisit a spark of brief happy ones. 'During one of my missions with the Guards, I encountered a rather unique Spanish mechanic.'

'Miguel,' Abigail smiled.

'He was getting hassled by a group of bullies calling him, "four eyes" and "tubby" while he was building a car in his garage. I approached them, knocked out the leader, and the rest ran off and never bothered him again.' Ryan smiled as he remembered. 'He built several tools and gadgets that really bailed me out on some of those missions. And when I needed somewhere to go, angry and alone with my sister to look after, Miguel was there, only too happy to take us in to live with him.'

Abigail's heart was warmed by the thoughts of there still being kindness and goodwill in the world of today.

'That was my life… no, our life during most of the pandemic. We stayed in, watched movies, did what we had to do, and I continued to look into my family fire.' Ryan's face darkened again. 'Then a few weeks ago my life fell apart, all over again.'

Abigail could already guess. 'Something happened Jessica.'

'Jess and I were walking to the supermarket when I was knocked out by a guy in a hoody with his head down. I remember a struggle, then waking up alone on the footpath by myself, no Jess.'

'Didn't someone see it happen?'

'We were walking by ourselves.'

The two sat in silence for a few minutes.

'Jessica is the only family I have left,' Ryan was starting to get emotional. 'She means everything to me. I've been trying to find her ever since she went missing. I nearly lost hope... until Mr. Mulrua sent me this email.' Ryan showed the email to Abigail, who gasped.

'So he knew?'

'He knew something alright, and someone killed him before he got the chance to tell me.'

'Ryan, why are you so convinced the email was genuine, that it wasn't some hoax or a joke?'

'I never said I was, but I've had nothing else to go off since Jessica went missing. I knew Mulrua had solid credentials so it seemed enough to give a shot.'

'This is insane.'

'I know.'

'I mean... really insane.'

'You're not going to go home though.'

'Not a chance in hell.'

Ryan smiled. 'Thank you Abigail,'

'Let's go find Jessica.'

16

Ryan and Abigail left the pool area and went back up the stairs to their hotel room. It had just gone half past eleven and the hotel had quietened down greatly to the point where the receptionists were twiddling their thumbs looking at the computer. Back in the room, Miguel had already fallen asleep in bed with the computer left out on the table.

'He never stops' laughed Ryan. 'Always doing a bit of programming, a bit of fixing. It's his life.'

Abigail looked at the computer. 'He was looking at sites on ways to fix engines.'

Ryan shot around and stared at the computer. 'Shit! I forgot when we used the turbo boost earlier it must've blown the engine. Miguel's obviously trying to figure out a way to fix it.'

Abigail noticed Ryan was a little worried. 'Everything ok?'

'Yeah no, it's ok, just means we can't make a quick escape if-'

Ryan was cut off by the familiar sound of sirens from outside, and this time there were more of them.

Panic started appearing on Ryan and Abigail's faces.

'Miguel!' Ryan shouted shaking him in bed. 'C'mon get up!'

'Wha… Wh… What's going on?' Miguel asked groggily.

'Police are back.' Ryan replied tensely.

'Crap! The truck is still busted. We can't go. We're stuck.'

Ryan began processing the options. The truck was broken. There was no way they could outrun them on foot. He still had no appetite to turn himself in… Unless…

'We're going to turn ourselves in.'

'Excuse me?!' Miguel and Abigail both said at the same time.

'There's no point continuing to run. You both said earlier that I can't avoid them forever. So I'm not going to. What I will do, is try to find the case file on Mulrua's death, see if there are any leads, they might be the best way of linking Mulrua's death to Jessica's disappearance.'

Miguel and Abigail didn't look overly convinced. 'Ok,' Abigail started. 'A - how are you going to get to the case file if we're under arrest. B - Even if you do find the case file, how do you know there's going to be anything useful? And C - How the hell do you plan on escaping if you do find said information considering they think you're.. no WE are the killers?'

Miguel was of a similar mindset. 'I agree with Scouse, Ryan have you thought this through?'

'A little bit, plus I don't see anyone with a better idea.'

Abigail and Miguel exchanged nervous glances.

'I need you to trust me, guys.'

Abigail maintained her nervous expression. She certainly wasn't convinced this would work. But as Ryan rightly pointed out, there weren't many options.

'Ok, let's do it.' She replied.

'Miguel?' Ryan asked.

Miguel rolled his eyes. '*Por Amor de Dios,* alright I mean how bad can it be? I'm sure the food will be good.'

At that moment, the door was knocked down and several Guards flooded into the hotel room.

'Ryan Striker, Abigail Davies, and Miguel Gutierrez you're all under arrest!'

17

Thrown into the back of a Garda car, Ryan, Abigail, and Miguel were taken to the Garda headquarters in Drogheda. It was grey and dull on the outside, and not a whole lot better on the inside. The station was poorly lit, and the paint colour was dark and dreary. While being guided handcuffed in a corridor towards their cell, Abigail whispered to Ryan.

'So, what's the plan here Ryan?' she asked. 'How are you going to get the case file?'

'I'll be the first one interviewed,' Ryan responded. 'After I'm done, I'll lose the Guards and go to where they keep the case files. If I find the file on Mulrua, then we escape.'

'Ok, and what about us?'

Ryan observed her with a confused look. 'Excuse me?'

'All you said was what YOU, are going to do, you never explained what myself and Miguel are supposed to do.'

Ryan maintained his puzzled look. 'Sit tight in the cell and wait for me.'

Abigail looked annoyed. 'And what if they try to interview us?'

'Don't tell them anything incriminating.'

Miguel rolled his eyes.

'Right, you into this cell.' One of the Guards said pointing at Miguel. They were bog-standard at best, containing only a single bed, tv, toilet, and a plain white table. The Gard said the same to Abigail who was put in the cell beside him. 'Striker, follow me, Superintendent Rafferty wants to speak to you.'

Ryan's ears perked up. 'Would that be a Superintendent JASON Rafferty?'

'Just follow me,' the Guard replied.

'Be back soon,' Ryan said to Abigail and Miguel with a wink.

Abigail was fuming. 'Did that clown think for a second about us while thinking up this wonderful plan that probably won't work?'

'Yeah, he's not great when it comes to leading and inspiring' Miguel agreed.

Ryan followed the Guard down the hallway towards a big office with a section of seats outside. It was situated on the second floor at the corner of the police station.

'Sit down,' the Guard demanded. 'Superintendent Rafferty will see you soon.'

'Any chance of a book to read?' Ryan asked nicely. 'Maybe a cup of tea?'

The Guard walked off and ignored him. Ryan sat in silence for a few minutes before hearing some commotion from further down the opposite corridor.

'I didn't know she was an old lady alright! I thought she had stolen my wallet!' Two officers appeared around the corner and were dragging an African-Irish man with them. He was about Ryan's age, bald, with a thick brown beard, and looked incredibly strong. Almost as if he'd been born in a gym and slept every night on a bench under a barbell. He was wearing a stringy skin-tight vest and didn't look best pleased to be thrown in a chair beside Ryan.

'Sit down and shut up, Lovell!' One of the Guards shouted. 'We'll deal with you later.'

The two walked off, leaving Ryan alone with this Lovell, who happened to be smiling to himself.

'What ya in for bro?' he asked.

'Main suspect in a murder investigation apparently. You?'

'Beating up a old lady.'

'Not very chivalrous.'

'It wasn't my fault bro, my wallet was stolen last night and I spent all this morning looking for it until I saw someone with one the exact same design as mine.'

'And this happened to be an old lady?

Lovell looked uncomfortable, 'She was very tall for an old lady.'

Ryan smiled to himself. 'What's your name?'

'Dynamite,'

Ryan's eyes narrowed. 'Excuse me?'

'Well, my real name is Joel Lovell, but I prefer to go by Dynamite.'

Ryan kept his amused look. 'I think I'll stick to Joel. Name's Ryan Striker.'

Joel's eyes widened. 'Woah you're the guy from the news! Brah, you're not being arrested are ya?'

'It's certainly not in the plan, although I do need questions answered.'

'Hope it works out bro, always hate seeing innocent people go to jail for no reason.'

Ryan turned and looked at him inquisitively.

'You don't think I did it?'

At that moment someone opened the office door and shouted. 'Ryan Striker!'

'That's me,' Ryan rose from his seat and began walking towards the office.

'Trust me bro,' Joel asserted before Ryan went in. 'I've been around long enough to know a killer when I see one. And I definitely don't see a killer in you.'

18

Ryan sat opposite Jason Rafferty in his office. The office wasn't much different from the way Ryan remembered it. The office was darker and the walls needed a good paint job. There was an overwhelming smell of coffee in the room, which matched up with the three mugs on Rafferty's desk and the many more in the overflowing bin beside the desk.

'Love what you've done with the place,' Ryan opened. 'The walls in particular really show off your brighter side.'

Rafferty stared him down.

'What were you doing in Callystown the morning of Michael Mulrua's murder?' Rafferty asked.

'I needed to speak with him.'

'Yes, we know you had a meeting arranged.' Rafferty replied irritably. 'About what?'

Ryan sat in silence.

'Look Striker, we need to catch this killer, media pressure is building and the family wants answers, we have no leads, and no evidence was pulled from the crime scene. We need help.'

Ryan folded his arms and smiled. 'Well, what do you know? 'Chief Superintendent and still asking me for help. Still looking for me to bail you out. How did you survive all these years without me?'

'This has nothing to do with us Striker!' Rafferty shouted. 'This is to do with finding the killer of an innocent man. Now I know you know something. I know it's no coincidence that the first time you show up in years someone ends up dead. Now I am giving you one last chance to talk!'

Ryan maintained his composure. 'Do you think I killed him?'

Rafferty didn't blink. 'No, I don't.'

'So why am I here?'

'Because I believe there's a reason why you went to Callystown that morning. I know you a lot better than you think Striker, I know what makes you tick.'

'Enlighten me then Rafferty, Why do you think I was there?'

Rafferty looked him right in the eyes. 'When you were with us, the only thing that kept you going on missions was providing for Jessica and figuring out what happened to your family. You didn't care about money or fame or anything. So I believe you went to Mr. Mulrua that day in the hope of finding another clue. Perhaps he knew something of interest about the fire. Only as you arrived he was dead.'

Ryan smiled. 'Did you have Sherlock Holmes helping you with that?

'Or something happened Jessica.'

Ryan's expression darkened which gave Rafferty all he needed.

'Told you I knew how you tick. So something has happened to her.' Now it was Rafferty's turn to smile despite himself. 'What happened to her Ryan?'

The mood changed instantly.

'Stay the hell out of this Rafferty!' Ryan roared across the table. 'My sister is absolutely no concern of yours.'

'This could all be over if we just worked together.' Rafferty pleaded.

'It would already be over if you hadn't lied to me all those years ago in the first place. We're done here.' Ryan rose from his seat and walked toward the door.

'I'm trying to give you an out Ryan,' Rafferty shouted. 'I want this over just as much as you do. You help me. I can help you find Jessica.'

Ryan opened the door and turned to look Rafferty in the eye. 'All you want is to protect your reputation. That's all you've ever cared about. It was all that mattered to you when you pretended to care about me and my sister. So take that offer and shove it right up your ass. I'll have this case solved long before you finish your fiftieth daily coffee.' Ryan slammed the door behind him leaving Rafferty in the room alone stunned.

'Well,' Rafferty thought. 'Least I have something to go on now.' He had a lot of things running through his mind, a lot of thoughts, yet there was one overriding feeling he felt.

Guilt.

19

A policeman was waiting for Ryan outside Rafferty's office. 'C'mon Striker, back to the cell,' he muttered. He put Ryan's hands behind his back and pushed him forward.

Ryan knew that the evidence room was on the second floor and all cells were kept in the basement. He had to stay on this floor. As they walked toward the stairs Ryan noticed a changing room to the side and had an idea.

Ryan knocked his head back against the policeman's face to stun him, then reached for his pocket and whipped out a cloth that he firmly pressed against the policeman's mouth, within a few seconds the policeman was asleep.

'Valerian,' Ryan smiled, 'Always does the trick.' Miguel had told Ryan about valerian a few years ago. It was a herb native to Europe and parts of Asia. People commonly used it for sleep disorders and insomnia. When Ryan was having sleepless nights thinking about his family fire, he took mild doses to help him fall asleep. Later Ryan used it on some of his missions, which came in handy when trying to sedate people. He pulled the policeman into the changing room where he stole the clothes and walked out disguised as a policeman. Only a few policemen were walking around the corridors so it was easier for the disguised Ryan to get into the evidence room. The room was full of drawers containing case files so it took Ryan a while to find the Michael Mulrua one. Eventually, Ryan took it out and flicked through the contents. The file had background checks, post mortem results, but nothing that Ryan didn't already know, except... Ryan noticed something in Mr. Mulrua's background check. It was an article from the local newspaper.

CALLYSTOWN CROOKS CAUGHT

7th September 1984

Local authorities confirmed today the arrest of the local street gang responsible for several recent break-ins and robbery attempts. The gang had been responsible for the theft of twenty-thousand Irish pounds over the past two years.

Ryan began speed-reading the article due to time constraints but the picture in the middle of the article caught his attention. There were four young guys in the picture with their names given just below.

From left to right- Carl Hoban, Niall Swords, Pauric O'Flynn, and Michael Mulrua.

Ryan's heart began to race. So Mr. Mulrua wasn't always the kind understanding principal everyone knew and loved. He was once a petty thief as a youngster. Ryan took the news report and quietly left the evidence room.

Suddenly, the alarm went off and a voice came on the intercom. '*Warning! Security Breach on 2nd Floor. Suspect is wearing a police uniform, five ft eleven, and potentially armed.*'

'There he is!' Ryan turned to the left of the corridor and saw two policemen racing towards him at full speed.

'Looks like the Valerian wore off,' Ryan muttered to himself. He turned and bolted down in the opposite direction towards the lift. Miguel and Abigail were still in the basement, so he needed to get back down there and get them out safely and quickly. Ryan remembered their cell wasn't too far from a nearby exit. If Rafferty had heard word of a security breach he would've phoned for reinforcements from other stations. As Ryan thought through the steps in his head he remembered what Abigail had said to him earlier. 'Maybe I didn't think this through properly,' he thought.

The lift was at the right of the corridor and Ryan was nearly there. The Guards however were gaining on him. Ryan could hear the sounds of their footsteps getting louder and faster. He could hear the lift ahead of him begin to close. With all his effort he just managed to get into the lift before it closed, going at such a pace he couldn't decelerate quick enough before crashing into the back of the lift. The doors closed just before the Guards could reach in and grab him. Ryan slumped against the back to catch his breath and think about the article.

How did the article relate to why Mulrua was killed? Of course, it may have just been a coincidence and the police were just looking at different avenues for a motive. Yet, it was a new lead that Ryan didn't have before he had stepped back into the world of police when he turned himself in.

'Didn't take me long to piss someone off again,' Ryan smiled to himself. The lift hit the bottom floor and Ryan slowly picked himself up off the floor. The lift door slowly opened and Ryan quietly approached the door. He'd been dropped off outside the entrance to the prisoner's cell section. There were no Guards surprisingly, perhaps they had all raced towards the second floor in the evidence room. Ryan took a quick look around before stealthily moving towards Abigail and Miguel's cells.

'Guys, I'm back,' Ryan muttered as he knocked on both doors.

'Took you long enough,' Abigail groaned.

'Find anything worthwhile?' Miguel asked.

'Something we didn't already know that could be of interest, which I consider a success.' Ryan chirped.

'Something that could explain why he had to die? Because I would hate it if your master plan had fallen to pieces because it wasn't thought through properly.' Abigail asked sarcastically.

'Oh Abigail,' Ryan drawled. 'Relax. We have something to go off now which we didn't have before and we're right beside an exit.'

'Ryan, do you have keys?' Miguel asked.

Ryan reached into his pockets and dug around for a few seconds, before looking up at Abigail and Miguel slightly embarrassed.

'There's none here,' Ryan admitted.

Miguel's head dropped and Abigail gave him a death stare. 'So how the hell do you intend on getting us out?'

Ryan looked at his two friends and was kicking himself that he hadn't a notion of how to open the doors. But he had to appear confident.

'I'll think of some-'

'Freeze!'

Ryan turned and looked at the entrance, which was now blocked by two Guards. They both had guns pointed.

20

'Put your hands above your head and turn around!' one of the Guards shouted. Ryan did as told and went up against the wall.

'Any new ideas?' Abigail asked sarcastically from inside the cell.

'Still trying to think of a few.' Ryan replied unenthusiastically.

'You all need to-' one of the Guards started talking again before the sound of one of them hitting the floor was heard followed by the sound of a taser. Ryan, Abigail, and Miguel spun around to see Joel Lovell standing above the two Guards on the floor with a taser in his hand.

'I want in!' Joel shouted enthusiastically.

Ryan looked stunned. 'Excuse me?'

'Yo, all that drama between you and Rafferty? I love me a good mystery. I wanna help out.'

Abigail and Miguel just stared at him.

'Ryan, who is this?' Miguel asked.

'Dynamite' Joel responded.

Ryan rolled his eyes. 'No, he's... uh... a guy I met before talking to the Chief Superintendent.' 'Abigail, Miguel, meet Joel Lovell.'

'You need keys?' Joel asked.

'Yeah, because Mr. Forgetful here didn't realise that cell doors don't open themselves,' Abigail said, looking at Ryan with her head cocked to the side.

Joel squatted down and searched the Guards pockets. Thankfully, one of them had the keys. 'Catch!' shouted Joel who tossed them to Ryan.

Ryan nodded in appreciation and turned to open the cell doors letting Abigail and Miguel out.

'Good to see you amigo,' smiled Miguel. He turned to Joel and gave him a fist bump.

'Fair play for tasering the Guards, that takes some serious finesse.'

'Joel Lovell is full of finesse,' Joel answered in a deliberately deeper voice. 'He fears no man and lives life on the edge.'

'So you're not called Dynamite?' Abigail asked looking at him.

'Not exactly honey,' Joel smiled with a wink. 'But I am dynamite in lots of ways.'

'OK!,' Ryan said loudly before Abigail could do what her infuriated face suggested she might if she had the chance. 'Joel, thanks for covering my ass, you want in, your in. Now let's get out of here before someone else finds us.'

'Oh I also got us a ride,' Joel added. 'Friend of mine heard I was in trouble so I gave him a call.'

'Casually calling a mate in prison?' Abigail questioned. 'Ryan are you sure this is a good idea? This guy's mate could be a steroid dealer.'

'Hey baby, I'm all-natural. I look this beautiful due to elite-level genetics and a brutal training program.' Joel responded.

'We're gonna die' sighed Abigail.

'Joel, where's your guy?' Ryan asked, trying to shift the conversation to something less cringy. 'Outside the station?'

'Yeah c'mon let's go!' Joel walked past them towards the back of the room.

'I thought the exit was beside the lift?' Abigail asked.

'It is.' clarified Ryan before turning to look at Joel who was inspecting the tiles. 'What's going on Joel?'

'One of these here...' muttered Joel under his breath. 'Ahaa! This one here. You guys, listen.' He knocked on the two tiles he was closest to.

One gave off a normal sound, the other sounded… hollow.

Carefully, Joel lifted the tile off the floor revealing a hole in the ground.

'Here's your escape,' Joel said triumphantly.

'Impressive,' Ryan remarked.

'Ryan, a moment,' muttered Abigail in his ear before pulling him aside. 'How on earth do we trust this guy?'

'I mean he stopped us from being arrested and found us another way out. Is that not enough?' Ryan replied irritably.

'Funny because I thought that was your job. You were supposed to ensure this went smoothly but instead, you nearly got us into more trouble.'

Ryan opened his mouth to snap back but Abigail got the final words in. 'Must be easy to trust people when they can cover up your flaws.'

'You two done arguing so we can get out of here?' Miguel shouted while already climbing down the vent.

'Ladies first.' said Ryan gesturing towards the vent.

'Don't hurt yourself on the way down.' whispered Abigail patting him on the back. She walked towards the vent and climbed down. Ryan could hear more footsteps coming down the stairs and quickly moved down the vent himself while putting the tile back in place.

21

It was about a six-foot drop to the underground sewer where Ryan, Abigail, Miguel, and Joel landed. The cold and damp air whipped around them and gave off an uninviting atmosphere. It was as dark as the middle of the night with the only light coming through vents in the ceiling like the lampposts shining down on a poorly lit street. Empty Coke cans and other pieces of litter were lying around on each side of the path with a small stream of water in the middle. The tunnel was large enough for everyone to walk through, though there wasn't space for much more with the walls fairly enclosed.

'Right guys, my mate won't be too far, there should be regular vents on this path up to the surface.' Joel took a look down the tunnel. 'If I remember correctly he told me to take the tenth vent on this path.'

'Wait, how does he know the layout of the sewers?' Abigail asked.

'I can add to that, how the hell did he know where that exit was?' Miguel quizzed.

'Guys, let's walk and talk.' Ryan urged looking at the ceiling. 'We still have police on our tail.'

They started walking in a single file due to the narrowness of the tunnel.

'He's a funny guy to be fair.' Joel spoke thoughtfully as they walked. 'Walks up to me in the street one day and asks me to do him a favour. To wander about and report any scraps or trouble kicking off amongst young kids in my local area and to report them. In return, I get a nice little fifty euro note in cash straight into my hand every week.'

'What about knowing the layout of the sewers?' questioned Abigail.

'Dunno buttercup, he just gave the instructions when I called to tell him about our little spot of bother. See me being arrested happens a little more often than I'd like to admit.'

'Call me buttercup one more time and you'll be heading to a hospital before going back to jail.' threatened Abigail.

'Ooooh feisty, c'mon I'm only teasing ya.'

'What's this guy's name?' Ryan asked.

'Know very little about him, bro. Keeps himself to himself. We mostly communicate by email or WhatsApp. On the odd occasion I do meet him properly he has sunglasses and a baseball hat. Like he's trying to hide.'

'Can't wait to meet him.' Abigail muttered.

'This is the tenth vent guys.' Miguel noted as they approached it.

'Good stuff hermano' Joel acknowledged. 'Definitely didn't forget to count them.'

'I'll give you guys a boost up,' Ryan said, observing the distance between the ground and the vent. He boosted Abigail first, then Miguel, and finally Joel, who was quite the challenge given his heavyweight. The sun was beginning to set as they helped Ryan up to the surface. A cool breeze blew past them as their bearings. They had come out on a quiet street with little activity. The police station was about five kilometres behind them and there was no sound of Garda cars following them.

'I think we lost them,' puffed Miguel. He was red in the face and looked stressed.

'Everything ok?' asked a concerned Abigail.

'Yeah it's just... I generally don't have this much stress in my day-to-day life.' 'Normally it's staying at home working on programming and web designs.'

'Welcome to life in the fast lane.' Joel exclaimed with his arms extended. 'I live this life day in, day out. Chasing down bad guys, seducing beautiful women...'

'Assaulting old ladies?' Abigail asked with a sarcastic smile.

Joel's eyes widened and shot towards her. 'Who told you that?'

'Oh, just happened to overhear while sitting in my cell two lovely police officers talking about a self-centred, bald, immature narcissist who had just mistaken a retired female firefighter for a wallet thief.'

'That's why she was so tall!'

Ryan rolled his eyes. 'Joel where is our ride? I thought he was supposed to meet us here.'

A notification came in on Joel's phone just as Ryan asked. He took it out and read a text.

'He says he's two minutes away. Was held back with paperwork.'

'Paperwork?' asked a confused Ryan. 'What does this guy do for a living?'

'I think he used to be a Guard back in the day but left due to a falling out with one of his partners.'

Ryan's face began to darken. He was starting to suspect who Joel's mate might just be. It was then that a red truck pulled around the corner and parked in front of them. The driver got out and stood in front of them. He may have been a few years older, but Ryan recognized him instantly.

It was Andrew Keaton, Ryan's godfather.

22

You could feel the tension in the air as Ryan and Keaton locked eyes for the first time. Neither Miguel nor Abigail had known what Ryan's godfather looked like, although they found out quick enough. Keaton was tall and well-built, like Ryan himself. He was dressed in jeans and a sailor-neck sweater. His hair was reasonably short, tidy, and side-swept while on the fringes of turning grey. He wore sunglasses despite it coming close to sunset. Joel knew what he was talking about when he said that Keaton kept himself to himself.

'Hello Ryan,' Keaton nodded after a few moments. Ryan just stared him out of it. He wasn't going to forget what happened all those years ago. Abigail, fortunately, broke the silence.

'Hi there, my name is Abigail Davies. Joel here was telling us you could give us a ride away from the station? We are kinda in a bit of a hurry.'

Keaton kindly smiled back. 'Of course, there should be plenty of space in the back. He opened the side of the truck to let them all in. Joel and Miguel hopped in first, but Ryan was not moving, much to Abigail's disgust.

'If you want to stay and get arrested again that's fine. We aren't going to hang around. Swallow your pride and come on.'

Ryan took a deep breath and finally joined the others in the truck. Inside there were four seats with two facing each other. The floor was impeccably clean and the light inside the truck glistened off the seats. Clearly, very few people had been inside the truck if any. They drove for a few minutes in silence until Keaton spoke.

'Did you find your wallet Joel?' he asked with a smile on his face.

Joel squirmed uncomfortably. 'I didn't realize it was an old lady I jumped! And it wasn't even her who had it.'

'Don't worry kid. The bank cards it had were all PIN activated only. No one's going to steal any money.'

'You're one to talk about stealing from others Keaton,' muttered Ryan angrily.

Keaton looked into his rear-view mirror to look at Ryan. Observing the eyes Abigail noticed it was obvious Keaton was hurt and upset about what had happened. But the look began to turn serious and determined.

'So did you kids find anything that might tell us who killed Michael Mulrua?' Keaton's question surprised Ryan, Abigail, and Miguel. How would he have known what they were up to?

'I may not be part of the force anymore, but I still have contacts inside who keep me informed.

And they have had a lot to say about you three. Keaton observed them in his rear-view mirror. Jumping off Callystown secondary school, shooting at multiple Garda cars, and finally drugging and impersonating a security guard while being under arrest.'

Abigail, Miguel, and Joel all looked at Ryan who kept the same icy stare on Keaton.

'All this while being for the most part the one and only suspect in a murder investigation.'

'Do you know about the case?' asked Miguel.

'I do. From all the information I've gathered, Mulrua had no enemies, no reason for anyone to want him dead, and also there was no way in hell someone could have murdered him as the door was locked when Ryan arrived and no other way in or out.'

'Ryan you said you found something new in the evidence lock-up.' Abigail asked. 'Care to share?'

'I'm not sharing shit with him.'

With that, Abigail rolled her eyes, reached forward, and slapped Ryan across the face as hard as she could. She did it so quickly that he couldn't even react to block.

Joel and Miguel sat there with their mouths open in stunned silence, while Keaton continued looking in the mirror with a smile starting to appear on his face. Ryan continued to look at Abigail, who equally matched his stare.

'Ryan if you want to find her again I suggest we investigate any potential leads we might have. Or perhaps I'll have to use a frying pan next time to knock some sense into you.'

'Damn, she's hot,' muttered Joel under his breath.

'What do you mean find her?' Keaton asked with a worried expression on his face.

'Ryan, what happened to Jessica?'

'I guess your contacts forgot to mention.' Ryan almost shouted. 'Jessica was kidnapped a few weeks ago while I was out walking with her.' The pain in Ryan's voice was obvious. Keaton dropped his eyes. 'I think her disappearance has something to do with Mulrua's murder. That's why I'm looking into it.'

'Tell us about what you found Ryan,' Miguel urged, hoping to kill the tension.

'When I was looking in the evidence room, I found a newspaper article from years ago of Mulrua being arrested with three others. Apparently, he was part of a group called 'the Callystown crooks.' They were robbers of some description.'

'I remember hearing about that gang back in the day' Keaton said. 'They were famous for breaking into houses and stealing anything of value, money, furniture, they were the best in the business.'

'However I understood there to be only three Callystown crooks, and Michael Mulrua wasn't one of them.'

Ryan reached into his pocket and took out the article. He showed it to Abigail, Miguel, and Joel before holding it in front of the mirror so Keaton could see it while driving.

'How were they caught?' asked Miguel.

'I don't remember it ever being clarified. But I think someone turned them in. The three guys were thrown in jail, no one heard about it again.'

'How would no one have picked up that Mulrua was once in a street gang?' Abigail wondered out loud. 'There has to be motive right there if he did.'

'Do we know anything about the other Callystown crooks now? Are they still alive, in jail maybe?' Miguel asked.

'They are all still alive as I understand it. They only served a few years, then got released.'

'We need to talk to the other crooks.' Ryan urged the others. 'Maybe they can share some insight as to what role Mulrua had with the Callystown crooks.'

'I don't know much about them in person but I do know someone who does.'

23

Daniel Swords, brother of Niall Swords lived in a housing estate not too far from where Keaton was now living himself. The houses were of modest size but all of them were kept in good shape. There were goals and playhouses in plenty of front gardens indicating many were inhabited by young families.

'I'm going to go see him.' Keaton hopped out of the truck. 'You guys stay here. Unless you want to get arrested again.' he warned. The others were locked in the back of the truck wondering how this connected to Mr. Mulrua.

'Do you guy's think there is a connection?' asked Joel. 'Between the crooks and Mulrua's murder?'

'Didn't Keaton say there was only supposed to be three though? And that Mulrua wasn't supposed to be one of them.' countered Abigail.

'More to the point, all this happened forty years ago. If someone had an agenda against them, why wait till now to act on it?' quizzed Joel.

'And what does this have to do with Jessica?' gritted Ryan. The other three turned towards him with sympathy. 'Mulrua said he knew what happened to her, that he had known for a while, and that he had made many mistakes before.'

'Why not just tell in the email? Why call you into the school?' Joel asked.

'I know I said it before Ryan but I wasn't kidding when I said Mr. Mulrua never held meetings like that. And as good of a principal as he was, he rarely admitted when he made mistakes.' confirmed Abigail.

'Maybe he was feeling guilty? Maybe he was having flashbacks to forty years ago where he was spending his days robbing people for him and his friends benefit.' offered Miguel.

'What if it wasn't for their benefit?' Ryan suddenly raised his head. 'What if they were using that money for something good?'

'I dunno bro, last I heard stealing that amount of money isn't good or morally right.' Joel muttered sadly.

'When would it be though?' Gears were starting to turn in Ryan's head. 'When would you guys try and steal two grand and consider it the right thing to do?'

'Ryan, it's never the right thing to steal, have you forgotten the 8th Commandment?' Miguel reminded.

'Obviously, objectively it isn't.' Ryan acknowledged. 'But what if you genuinely believed you were doing the right thing by stealing that money and if you didn't, you would regret it for the rest of your life?'

'I'm still lost bro,' Joel shook his head.

'No, I'm starting to get you. C'mon guys why would you steal that amount of money and justify it?'

'I mean if I was in debt and needed to pay some guys off.' Miguel offered. 'I would have to try and get enough money.'

'Maybe you're not in debt but need to pay guys off for something else.' Ryan continued.

'Like what?' Joel asked.

'Something important, something so close to your heart that you can't live without it.' Ryan muttered frantically.

'Or someone,' Abigail added. She looked at Ryan and smiled.

'Now that's an idea.'

Just then the door opened and Keaton came back in. 'Right guys I think it's time to go back to my place. I've just heard a very interesting story.'

24

'I just spoke to Daniel Swords,' exclaimed Keaton who pulled out of the estate. 'Apparently, back in the 80s the crooks weren't stealing money for their own benefit, but rather to raise money for Carl Hoban's sister who'd been abducted.'

Abigail, Miguel, and Joel all shot their eyes at Ryan, who continued to listen attentively.

'Mary Hoban was abducted on August the 1st 1984, the kidnappers sent the Hoban family a ransom note demanding twenty-thousand for her release.'

'That is hefty.' muttered Miguel.

'So Carl went to his three best friends to come up with a plan to raise twenty-thousand themselves. That plan was to loot from other families in the area.'

'Mulrua was one of the friends.' confirmed Abigail.

'They were a great success for a while.' Keaton continued. 'They would meet every Friday night and loot a house for any cash they could find., all while being motivated by the fact they'd be able to raise the money to save Carl's sister.'

'Did they not alert authorities?' asked Abigail. 'Why immediately resort to theft?'

'The parents did alert police, but they were advised that the best chance of getting their daughter back was to raise the money themselves. Which was monumentally difficult back then. Carl's father was an industrial worker earning about one pound, one pound forty an hour for forty-two hours a week. Not exactly going to raise twenty-thousand in a hurry.'

'So Carl took matters into his own hands,' Abigail deduced.

'They would have succeeded, but one of his friends got cold feet and ended up spewing the story to the police.

They were caught immediately and sent to jail. Except for the one who tipped the police off.'

'Michael Mulrua,' Ryan smiled.

'The very same,' continued Keaton. 'He came from a very powerful family who were able to pull the strings to keep him out of jail.'

'And the other three?' asked Joel. 'Surely they got some leniency because of why they were stealing?'

'Nope. Police came under pressure from the families they stole from to take action. The money was returned and that was that.'

'What happened to Mary?' Abigail asked.

'She was never found.'

The other four bowed their heads simultaneously.

'Mary was adored by the whole community, pretty, popular, and friendly.

Apparently, she broke her arm a few weeks before and was going to spend a few months in a cast, which only deepened Carl's concern for his sister.'

'So the money was just returned to the families?'

'Yep, that was the end of that.'

Keaton had finished the story and continued to drive, leaving Ryan, Abigail, Miguel, and Joel to ponder.

'So how the hell does this fit into what's happening today?' exclaimed Joel.

25

It took them another ten minutes to reach Keaton's house which stood on its own on a hill looking onto Callystown beach. It was a clear night, and the light of the moon reflected off the sea like there was a party going on under the water.

'Never knew you lived so remotely boss,' noted Joel as he took in the surroundings.

'I like to keep a low profile. This place is quiet, helps me think.' Keaton responded. He opened the door and lead the others into what looked like a lift door under his stairs.

'What is this?' laughed Joel. 'You have a Batcave or something?'

'Not exactly,' Keaton smiled.

He opened the gate and let the others in.

'Why did you leave the police force, Keaton?' asked Ryan. The tension in the air as Ryan spoke could be felt by everyone. 'Why come the whole way out here to live by yourself?' Keaton flicked the switch on the wall and the lift began to descend.

'When I was with the Guards and especially towards the end of my time there were certain things I didn't see eye to eye on with my colleagues which became apparent. When that became a big enough problem, I went and pursued my own goals myself. I bought this place from a guy who was looking to retire to the sunshine in Lanzarote and turned the basement into my own private office.'

As they hit the bottom the door opened and they were greeted by a truly incredible sight. The lift dropped them on a narrow metal pathway with stairs going down to a massive open area. It was wide, large, and had a dark mysterious vibe to it.

There were computer screens hooked up against the walls with keyboard consoles sticking out. In the middle was a round table with a pole in the centre connected to the ceiling that was emitting a greenish light. Keaton smiled as the others looked on in disbelief.

'This used to be an underground train station.' Keaton explained. 'Before the previous owner came in and did it up. We have CCTV cameras all over Callystown. I generally use it to keep an eye on street gangs and other various trouble-makers.'

'I've never seen anything like it.' exclaimed Abigail in disbelief.

'And the technology,' stammered a giddy Miguel. The station was full of different cables, pieces of metal, and alloys lying around. 'Think of the things we could do with this, the things we could build!'

Joel noticed a little fridge beside one of the desks and quickly while no one was watching moved over and took a look inside when his mouth dropped. It was packed to the brim with Guinness cans. 'I gotta get a party down here sometime,' he thought to himself. He had always been a passionate fan of Guinness and regularly drank cans of it when going out, or when just needing to let loose, but mostly just to let loose.

'So you've been living here all this time?' asked a confused Ryan. They all turned and looked at Keaton, who sighed and began explaining.

'I have always been passionate about pursuing justice, putting bad guys behind bars, and helping out the little guy. For years that goal was fulfilled by working with the police. However, a few years back I noticed a trend, crime amongst young people were starting to rise among twelve to fifteen-year-olds.

Minor stuff sometimes, shop-lifting, bullying, but that was escalating to further violence. Harassment, drug dealing, torturing. We couldn't keep up as we didn't have enough officers at the time, and the Superintendent didn't consider it a big enough problem to take our attention away from the main adult crimes, but it kept getting bigger.' Keaton paused for a moment before continuing. 'Things changed when a young kid walked into my office with his little sister having just lost his parents. In his eyes, I saw the same thing I saw in myself. The determination to pursue justice, the thirst for adventure and excitement.' He sadly smiled and looked at Ryan. 'Your father was my best friend Ryan. I was honoured he trusted me to take care of you and Jessica.'

Ryan maintained his stare. He wasn't going to give any emotion away.

'You wanted to do your bit to help Ryan.

So, I was able to convince the Superintendent to let us train you to become someone who could go out and stop the minor incidents of bullying and shoplifting. Soon, you became someone who was stopping gangs and saving people's lives. You slowed the youth crime rate down to the point where it was almost non-existent.'

'Sounds unreal bro,' said a very impressed Joel. 'Respect.'

'Except we had made a deal,' Ryan reminded him. 'You didn't keep your end of the agreement.'

'I never meant it to get as far…'

'You used me to impress your Superintendent!' Ryan shouted. 'You knew for months that my parent's case file had been closed and still, you sent me out for your own benefit!'

'I didn't do it just for my benefit Ryan.' Keaton argued calmly. 'Yes, I wanted to impress my superiors, yes, I didn't want to break the news to you.

But I also wanted to stem the tide of the problem you were so good at stopping. You were happy at what you were doing, you had a home, you were earning money. I thought by telling you we had stopped searching you would lose interest, go down the wrong road.'

'You didn't have to lie,' gritted Ryan.

'You didn't have to run away kid.' Keaton responded.

The two continued to lock eyes on each other. Tension was starting to build.

Finally, Abigail spoke.

'Look, what's done is done, neither of you can change what happened. Right now there's still a killer on the loose who has to be caught. Both of you also have someone special who is still missing. Both of you seem like people who want to do the right thing. As far as I'm concerned, that's enough for the pair of you to work together.'

'We know Mulrua turned in the other crooks. I think there's a clear motive there.' Miguel commented. 'I also don't think it's a coincidence that someone's sister was abducted forty years ago and now this time someone else's sister was abducted.'

'The email Mulrua sent Ryan hints at having made a lot of mistakes and that he knows what happened to Jessica. It sounds like he is maybe referring to alerting the police about the crooks as one of his regrets.' Joel added.

'I still have a funny feeling about that email Ryan. I've said it before he was not one for admitting he was wrong. Yes, he was a nice guy and all, but totally full of himself and arrogant also.'

'What are you saying Abigail?' Keaton asked.

'I'm saying it doesn't make sense he would have a sudden change of heart like this for no reason. And as soon as the email is sent he's murdered? It almost seems… staged'

'You mean you think...' Keaton pushed.

'I don't think Mr. Mulrua sent that email, I think the killer did.'

26

'That is so insane it might actually be right.' Miguel exclaimed. 'I have never liked coincidences with murders and that would explain the coincidence.'

'He kidnaps Jessica, sends the email to get Ryan involved, then murders Mulrua to... frame him?'

'No.. not to frame me. To get me involved.' Ryan muttered. 'By sending me the email and placing me at the scene of the crime, he's made me a main suspect and he's forcing me to get involved in the case.'

'Why do that? Why you?' Miguel asked.

'Can I just make the point that we still haven't a clue who our guy might be?' reminded Joel, who had already cracked open a can of Guinness and was sipping away. 'Isn't that where we should be looking?'

'Ok well, there are plenty from forty years ago who lost out big when the crooks were arrested.' Abigail mentioned. 'Namely the other three crooks.'

'As per my understanding, they are still alive.' Keaton responded.

'Can we talk to them?' Ryan asked.

'No chance. Remember you guys are wanted for breaking out of prison.' Keaton reminded.

'So we're stuck here?'

'I think it's best if you keep a low profile until we're confident we have the guy. If you go out… you risk getting caught again.'

'What will you do boss?' asked Joel.

'I need to go out and do some more digging myself. Also, to finish some paperwork.'

Miguel noticed a series of sheets with text lying on the table in the middle of the hall. He took a quick look at the sheets and looked at Keaton.

'What's all this?' he asked. They had titles like *Number of crime incidents amongst young people in 2024* and *Impact of COVID-19 on young people*

Keaton noticed the sheets and sighed. 'That is the bones of the plan I wanted to propose to the Garda Commissioner.'

'What plan?' quizzed Abigail.

'It's a long story,'

'Well, it looks like we've got the time to listen to it,' Joel acknowledged.

'Ok then,' Keaton sighed before beginning his story. 'About ten years ago when I was still with the Guards we started to notice the upward trend in young adult crime. It gradually grew year after year before skyrocketing in 2018, the year you joined Ryan.' Keaton nodded at Ryan who was listening attentively.

'When we had Ryan the curve began to flatten and things were looking up again, but after Ryan left things got worse. Once the pandemic hit in 2020 and in the years ensuing, young adult crime rates shot up in a way I never thought possible.'

'You had left the police force at that stage.' Ryan argued. 'Why did it matter to you?'

'You can take the cop out of the job but you can't take the job out of the cop.' Keaton smiled. 'I conducted some research as to why things were going so bad. And the answer I kept coming back to was COVID.'

The four looked at each other and knew what was coming next.

'For two years young people missed out on so much during COVID, holidays, school, social gatherings, first dates.

Some had lost close family members and some had fallen so far behind in schoolwork on Zoom that they just gave up and fell off the radar.

It led to a certain cohort feeling bitter, angry, heartbroken over what they had lost.'

The other four looked at each other and knew they were all thinking the same thing. Each of them had hated the pandemic period and certainly felt their own anger over what they had lost.

'My age and other age groups obviously still missed out on loads, but looking back, it was the younger cohort who suffered the most. And now it's still a problem that our police force can't tackle on their own.'

'On their own?' Miguel pushed.

'I came up with the idea of developing a team of young people, working closely with the Guards to tackle this problem. All members would be hungry, enthusiastic, have special skills, but above all else be able to understand why those engaged in the crime were doing so and help in a way people like me, just can't.'

Miguel continued to look through the papers. 'Has the idea been proposed yet?'

'I can't go ahead until I have a set of young people to form a team. For the last few months, Joel has done a pretty good job. But I need more people with different skillsets. Like computing,' he nodded at Miguel.

'Wait wait…' Abigail stuttered 'You want *us* to do this?'

'If you want to… I think the four of you could be a great starting point.'

'Has this little team of yours got a name?' sneered Ryan.

'Actually, I did have one in mind.' Keaton nodded *'Strikerback'*

Ryan's eyes widened and his face almost began to twitch.

'In my head, the name represents what I want the team to be about, young people striking back after their COVID years. To have their fun and excitement back by working with people who feel the same way.' Keaton bowed his head. 'I also wanted to name it after my best friend, Richard Striker.'

Ryan was breathing heavily like he was trying to compose himself.

Keaton was looking emotional himself. 'Right, I need to go. See you soon guys.' He quickly moved up the stairs and went out the door.

27

'You alright Ryan?' asked a concerned Miguel. Ryan still looked fairly shook up at the team name being after his dad.

'Yeah, yeah I'm fine thanks, Miguel,' answered Ryan who had already composed himself. 'Keaton was right, it won't be long before police end up finding us so we gotta figure out who killed Mulrua.'

'We can't ask anyone else about the Callystown crooks and we can't inspect either crime scene.' reminded Abigail.

'No, but we do have access to big kick-ass computers where we can do some digging.' Miguel smiled. He ran over to one of the desks with a keyboard. 'You guys do the theorizing, I'll do the research.'

'Ok so, our killer has to be connected to the original case forty years ago, so let's start there.' Joel suggested.

'Might one of the other crooks have killed Mulrua out of revenge?' offered Abigail.

'No, why wait forty years to do it? I'm sure they were angry, but if they were angry enough to kill, they would have done it there and then,' Ryan countered.

'Maybe they found something new out recently that triggered enough anger to kill. Something that wasn't known before?' Joel theorized.

'It was assumed the kidnappers killed Mary when they didn't take the money.' shouted Miguel looking at the computer. 'That's what was put down when the case closed.'

'So, maybe something else was discovered, someone discovered new evidence…. Ryan was thinking out loud. 'Miguel! Search up recent articles on Mulrua and see if you find anything.'

'Sí senor,' replied Miguel. 'Da da da... ahaa! Here's something, it's only a picture of Mulrua in his office. It looks like he's sponsoring a play in the town hall.'

'How recent is the photo?' asked Ryan walking over.

'A few months ago, This is the only Michael Mulrua public piece of content I could find.'

Ryan looked at the screen and studied it. He was certain Mulrua's death was linked to Mary Hoban's disappearance all those years ago. But something recent had to have aggravated the killer's anger to acting now and not before. Somewhere…

Then Ryan saw it.

It was there in the photo.

Hidden in plain sight.

'Oh my god…' Ryan muttered.

'What?' the other three shouted.

'But then who killed... why would he?... Ok, that answers some questions, and also opens more! But it would explain why Mulrua had to die now, in his office!'

'Holy shit bro, you haven't just solved it have you?' Joel stammered, almost choking on his can of Guinness.

'Not exactly, I might have a why, but not necessarily a who.'

Miguel and Abigail stared at the photo, then at each other.

'Do you see...?' started Abigail.

'No clue,' Miguel replied.

Just then Ryan's phone rang. He took it out and saw the caller ID was 'unknown.' It was an invitation to a video call.

'Miguel here, can you mirror this onto the big screen behind us?'

Miguel mirrored it and accepted the call. The four turned to the screen projector behind them and what they saw shocked them to the core. Ryan felt like he had been slapped and dropped to his knees.

Jessica Striker was sitting in front of them on the screen. Her mouth was covered and tears dripped down her face.

27

'Jessie,' Ryan stammered.

'Can you hear me, Ryan?' The voice at the other end was menacing and foreboding.

'Yes,' replied Ryan. His teeth were gritted and his whole body was shaking.

'So as you can see, I have your lovely sister in front of me.' 'She really is a delight Ryan. Never complained, always did as she was told… she is rather beautiful.' A hand appeared in front of the camera and began stroking Jessica's cheek.

'LET MY SISTER GO YOU PSYCHOPATH!!!' Ryan exploded, startling Abigail, Miguel, and Joel. His hands had smashed on the desk and his face was twitching in anger. Weeks of loneliness and heartache had boiled up in a few seconds. If he could have in that instant, he would have snapped the kidnapper's neck in pure rage.

'Now now, there is no need for that. I am merely here to propose a transaction.'

'Go on,' Ryan pushed.

'You want your sister back?' 'That is fair, I understand.' 'But it's going to come at a price, a price of twenty-thousand euros.'

Abigail, Miguel, and Joel glanced at each other. Was history repeating itself?

'You want to escape, don't you? Disappear, so you can get away with murder.'

'You figured that out huh? Smart guy. Yes, I do want to escape, and you want your sister back. I think it's a fair deal.'

'I also know why you did it, I saw the recent photo of Mulrua on the internet.'

The killer paused before responding. 'What does it matter?'

'I understand you're angry, I understand you want revenge, but this isn't the way.' Ryan was trying to talk him around.

'Shut up Striker, I don't want your sympathy, My offer is as it stands, In three hours' time, I want you at the abandoned Callystown gym hall with the twenty-thousand. You have the money, you get Jessica back if not...' A few seconds passed before a gun appeared at the edge of the screen pointed at the side of Jessica's head.

Abigail covered her mouth. Miguel dropped his eyes. Joel put his hands on his head.

'I want you and only you, should you bring anyone else, the trigger gets pulled.' *'See you soon Striker.'*

The call disconnected.

'I'm going to the bank,' muttered Ryan straight away walking towards the stairs.

'Hold on your not actually going to do as he says?!' exclaimed Abigail. 'What if he's lying?'

'Yeah well, I don't have much of a choice.'

'How the hell are you going to get twenty-thousand out in a few hours?!' exclaimed Joel.

'More to the point, do you even have twenty-thousand?' asked Miguel.

'Still trying to figure out the finer details guys!' shouted Ryan.

'Yeah, but if we come up with something maybe get some help…'

'Abigail, you heard what he said!' shouted Ryan. 'If there is anyone other than me he'd... Ryan almost started to cry. 'He said he would kill Jessica. I'm sorry guys but I can't risk that.'

'You're not alone anymore Ryan.'

Ryan turned and saw it was Miguel speaking this time.

'Ever since I met you you've always tried to do things on your own. From a very early age, you were in charge of protecting Jessica and doing what was right for her. You always did things alone, because there was no other option.' Miguel paused and looked to his left and right. 'But now, there are people here who really want to help, people who care about you, and... feel free to correct me if I'm wrong here guys, people who want some excitement in their lives again after coronavirus.'

Abigail and Joel smiled.

'I definitely want some action!' Joel shouted.

'There's no point telling me this is too dangerous.' Abigail warned. 'I already told you, Ryan I want some excitement in my life, I think *Strikerback* is the opportunity I've been waiting for.'

Ryan looked at the three people standing in front of him. The worried look on his face began to turn into a smile. He suddenly began to feel more confident.

'Ok then,' he paused and began to think. 'We're going to have to get money from somewhere, anyone got any ideas?'

'I think I can help you with that bro,' smiled Joel with a grin on his face.

<u>28</u>

It was fast approaching midnight when Ryan made his way towards the gym hall with a bag on his back with the money. The last few weeks had felt like years for him. He had missed Jessica and everything about her so badly since she went missing. Her smile, her laugh, her incessant need to sing at every opportunity purely to annoy him! He smiled as happy memories he had of Jessica came rushing back, but quickly reminded himself that those weren't going to be the last of his memories of her. He was, by hook or by crook going to see his sister again.

Was he scared? A little. His sister's life was resting in his hands. But as his friends reminded him, he didn't have to do things alone anymore.

The hall had been abandoned for a few years now. Once, it had been used as a stage for all local drama performances, yet as the new theatre had opened recently, it had become derelict. Patches of paint had fallen off the wall and cracks had started to appear in the windows. As Ryan approached the door he noticed it had been left slightly ajar. Pragmatically, he slowly pushed it open and peered inside. There was very little lighting with it being night-time and the main lights had been mostly blown out, but there was one light shining down on the centre of the room. It was shining down on a small figure in a chair.

Jessica.

She was handcuffed and had duct tape over her mouth, her face red from the incessant crying.

Ryan raced over and fell to his knees. First thing was to rip the duct tape off.

'Ryan...' Jessica whispered.

Ryan reached in and hugged his sister as tight as he could.

'I'm sorry Jessie... I'm sorry I couldn't come sooner.'

'So am I,'

Ryan spun around and saw the man who killed Mr. Mulrua and kidnapped his sister. He was pointing a gun at him.

It wasn't any of the Callystown crooks, this guy was younger, even as young as Ryan. He was wearing a worn shirt and jeans, he had bags under his eyes and looked like he hadn't slept in days, maybe even weeks.

'So you figured it out huh?' he sneered.

'Some of it,' Ryan replied. 'Other parts, I need you to fill in. Who you are might be a good start.'

'Liam Hoban' the man answered. 'Carl's son. I suppose you want the whole shebang though?'

'It would be nice.'

'The money first,' Liam pointed the gun at the bag Ryan had dropped on the ground.

Ryan picked up the bag and tossed it over to Liam, who opened it and confirmed Ryan had brought the money.

'Alright you've done enough chasing mate,' smiled Liam. 'I suppose we should start at the beginning.'

'Back forty years ago,' Ryan asked. 'Your aunt was abducted...'

'Not abducted!' snapped Liam. 'That was a lie! Evidence was presented and the police took it as fact without question. Mary Hoban was murdered!'

Ryan had thought as much when he saw the picture on the internet.

'Michael Mulrua murdered her didn't he?'

29

'Mulrua forged the kidnapper note and staged it to look like a kidnapping. He thought if he set the ransom price high enough, the Hoban family wouldn't be able to pay and it would explain why she was dead. But when Dad was close to raising the money, Mulrua turned him in to save his own neck, and bury his secret.'

'Why though?' pushed Ryan. He was trying to keep Liam talking, partly because he needed to stall, partly because he wanted to know.

'They were in love,' Liam answered. 'They were both in secondary school, from the same area, but Michael was abusive, violent, he even broke my aunt's arm!'

Liam was releasing years of built-up anger and still had the gun in his hand. Things were not over yet.

'Then one day he obviously...' Liam couldn't even mention it. 'Aunt Mary wasn't a strong woman, she lived in fear of him, too scared to tell anyone.'

'How do you know all this?' Ryan quizzed. 'I read the files in police storage, nothing about the two being acquainted.'

'My dad knew something was off about the case from the start, he spent a while digging, but it had already caused him too much heartache. His career went down the drain because he was arrested. After enough time he just gave up. But he passed the story down to me when I was fourteen and I have spent the last six years of my life trying to find the answer. A few years of isolating from the world helped out.'

'It's consumed you.' Ryan realised stepping back. 'It's driven you crazy.'

'WHAT WOULD YOU HAVE DONE STRIKER?!' Liam shouted. 'You see that's why I kidnapped Jessica there. You understand in a way that most don't. I know your history. All that time you spent trying to find out how your family died in that fire...' Liam paused for a moment. 'You see we're not all that different. We both believe in the correct course of justice. We both will do whatever it takes to get what we want. Admit it, you would have killed me right there and then when you saw I had Jessica. You wouldn't have listened to my side of why I took her.'

Ryan was listening attentively. He saw the deranged look in Liam's eyes. Yes, he got what he wanted, but at what cost? Suddenly, Ryan began to think of himself chasing and searching for the answers to his house fire. Would knowing really give him closure?

'I always suspected Mulrua was foul.' Liam continued. 'Even watching him as principal, I knew something was off, I was able to confirm my suspicions when I found Aunt Mary's diary while clearing out our attic. All the information was there. She wrote about the beatings, the threats, the fear. And the final entry the day before the ransom note turned up? She wrote and I quote, *I think Michael is going to snap.'*

Ryan remembered hearing that Mulrua once had serious anger issues. Never to this extent, however. 'You still had no proof though.' Ryan continued. 'You needed to prove that Mary was murdered and you needed a body.'

'I also needed an ally,' smiled Liam. I needed someone with a specific skill set, someone who had lost loved ones before, and someone who would take my side.'

'Me,' Ryan sighed.

'I mean your CV speaks for itself mate. Young hotshot cleaning up the streets, in cahoots with the police, but best of all, wounded, even more so as word on the street got out that you were betrayed by the people you worked for, the same people who betrayed my family.'

'Why kidnap Jessica?' Ryan asked with gritted teeth.

'A bargaining chip,'

'He tried to frame you Ryan,' spluttered Jessica from behind. 'He wouldn't stop talking about it. He was going to force the truth from Mulrua in his office, secretly record the confession, and…'

'Wait for you to walk in and allow you to make a simple choice, either you kill Mulrua yourself, or I shoot Jessica in the head right there and then.'

'You wanted *me* to kill him?' Ryan was shocked.

'C'mon you would have to admit it would have been a good plan.' sneered Liam.

'I wanted Mulrua dead but wasn't foolish enough to do it myself, so I would get you to do it and give myself time to escape. I would call the Guards, they arrest you for murder, but also my aunt would get the justice she deserved, Once I anonymously sent them the confession.'

'Sounds like you had it all figured out.' Ryan muttered. 'But you killed him. And I know why you did. Because you saw something you never expected to see in that office.'

Liam's eyes twitched in anger, he tried to speak but couldn't get the words out. Ryan knew he couldn't say it. It was so despicable that it drove him to commit murder.

'You saw your aunt's dead body.'

30

'The bastard... had the audacity to keep my aunt's skeleton in his office as a TROPHY!!!' screamed Liam. He was shaking in fury and at that moment Ryan genuinely felt sorry for him.

'The broken arm,' whispered Ryan. 'It was there and that was what gave it away.' Ryan had seen it in the photo Miguel found online. He knew he had seen it before, way back when he and Abigail found Mulrua dead in his office.

'I couldn't even look at him,' gritted Liam. 'I saw the knife on the desk he used to open letters, and the next few minutes were just a blur. I remember seeing him lying back in the chair, his shirt soaked in blood... the knife in my hand.'

Liam kept the gun pointed at Ryan but held out his left hand and looked at it like he was reminiscing about holding the knife. Ryan knew he had to keep him talking.

'So the plan went awry and you still had the proof, but the recording also proved you killed him.' Ryan was piecing the final pieces together. 'So you had to come up with a new plan. How on earth did you get out? There were no other exits.'

'I had just killed a respected principal with Guards on the way. I wasn't going to escape without cameras picking me up, so getting out wasn't going to be an option. So with no way out, I did the next logical thing.'

Ryan waited for the answer.

'I stayed at the scene of the crime'

31

'I noticed Mulrua had a hatch under his desk leading to a storage room where he kept some science equipment. It was the perfect hiding place. Thankfully it blended in with the rest of the floor's colour. The officers never suspected a thing.'

'And you must have worn gloves and a hat,' Ryan continued. 'So no fingerprints or hair fibres were found.'

'I still had to figure out my next move, and I remembered I still had one major bargaining chip.'

'Jessica.'

'And I was feeling nostalgic so I did the voice call looking for enough money to disappear, create a new identity and live the rest of my life knowing someone else would be able to piece everything else together when I left this.'

He reached into his pocket and took out the incriminating picture of Mulrua standing in the office and a red circle around the evidence.

'So I suppose that's that then Striker,' smiled Liam. 'Thank you so much for playing by the rules. Now you have your sister back and I can go free.'

'Yeah about that...' Ryan began. 'I can't let you go free.'

Liam's face began to darken. 'You do know I still have a gun in my hand?'

'True, but I've got a team.'

Ryan extended his arms out and waited only three seconds.

32

A few hours earlier, outside Superintendent Rafferty's office…

'Ok, remember the plan right?' Abigail was standing outside the door with Joel. 'We go in, explain what we know, and what we think we should do.'

'Can I say the line?' asked Joel.

'No jackass, do you want to piss him off even more?' snapped Abigail.

'For the shits and giggles?' laughed Joel. 'Oh absolutely.'

'We're trying to be professional here.'

'Abbie I can't even spell professional. I dropped out of school when I was like, six.'

'Just.. try to play it cool.' Abigail warned.

Joel gave her a wink.

'Ready?' she asked.

Joel nodded.

Abigail pushed open the door and the pair confidently strode in to see Rafferty sitting at his desk with Keaton standing with his arms folded leaning against the wall.

'Team *Strikerback* reporting for duty!' shouted Joel at the top of his lungs.

Angrily, Rafferty raised quickly to his feet. Keaton looked confused, but proud.

'You are all under arrest!' shouted Rafferty. 'Where's Striker?'

'Shut up Jason,' snapped Abigail. 'Ryan's gone to save his sister.'

'She was found?' exclaimed Keaton. Even Rafferty was showing interest beneath the anger.

They told Keaton and Rafferty about the voice call.

'Jason we have to get a team down there, it has to be the guy who killed Mulrua.' Keaton pleaded.

'All my guys are busy on other cases.' muttered Rafferty. 'Plus these are the same people who escaped custody only a few days ago, knocked out my officers, and tasered them! You think I'm going to believe a word of what they have to say?'

'Check your inbox lad, Miguel sent you a recording,' ushered Joel.

Rafferty took out his phone and sure enough, there was an email from Miguel's address. He opened the recording and put it on speaker for Keaton to hear.

Rafferty's expression darkened. 'Damn it, Ryan's gone there now?'

'Yes and we need your help,' pleaded Abigail. 'Listen, I appreciate we've been a nuisance and caused you the hassle.

But I think you two owe it to Ryan to give him any help he needs for saving his sister. After all, we all want to put this case to bed.'

Rafferty looked at Keaton. 'This the new project you're looking to propose?'

Keaton nodded.

Rafferty looked at the people in front of him and asked. 'Ok *Strikerback*, I'll give you all the help I can, you got a plan?'

'We have a plan.' Joel announced. 'And I suppose you could say it's… explosive.'

32

Back to the present…

'True, but I've got a team.'

Ryan extended his arms out and waited only three seconds.

'CUE THE EXPLOSIONS!!!' shouted Joel. He was standing on the second floor of the hall overlooking Liam and Ryan and began tossing mini sparklers down on top of Liam. The explosions were only minor and didn't harm him, but they caused enough surprise to knock him off balance. He dropped the gun and Ryan raced forward to rugby-tackle him to the ground. Rafferty and Keaton both sprinted in and managed to handcuff Liam from the ground allowing Ryan to get back on his feet. Trying to pull himself free, Liam muttered to Ryan,

'I ain't confessing shit in front of a judge Striker,'

'True,' Ryan smirked. 'But thankfully you already did. See this little thing on the jacket?' He pointed at the camera that had been put on the left of his jacket. 'Our whole conversation was recorded thanks to the techy genius of my mate Miguel Gutierrez. He's probably staring at you right now waving.'

Liam looked as if he had been slapped in the face.

'He's all yours gentlemen,' smiled Ryan.

Rafferty and Keaton pulled Liam away out of the hall leaving Ryan with Jessica. He turned and helped her untie herself before hugging her again.

'I thought I lost you.' Ryan was on the verge of tears.

'I never did,' smiled Jessica. 'I always knew you wouldn't give up. You never do.'

'Did he hurt you?'

'Nope, he never really cared about me that much, he just wanted justice for his family.'

'I love you so much Jessie,' smiled Ryan.

'I love you too big brother.'

The two continued to hug each other while Abigail and Joel quietly looked on from above.

'He needed that,' smiled Abigail. 'I can't imagine the stress he must've been feeling.'

'Me neither,' agreed Joel. 'So can we hug as well?'

Abigail shot him an icy stare. 'In your dreams.' she snarled before heading for the stairs.

'Had to try,' Joel thought to himself.

33

The sun began to rise over Callystown for the new day by the time Keaton and Rafferty arrived back after making the arrest. They found Ryan, Miguel, Joel, and Jessica all standing around talking about the crazy past few days. Abigail was talking with her parents, but quickly joined when she saw Rafferty and Keaton approach.

'Well, isn't this a fun group?' smiled Rafferty as he approached them. 'Care to fill me in on the whole story one more time? Two murders in one are a lot to get your head around.'

The others looked at Ryan, believing he should be the one to explain the story.

'Carl Hoban gave up on finding the truth behind his sister's disappearance years ago. But that didn't stop Liam from looking into it himself.

At some point, he found Mary Hoban's diary which alluded to violence between herself and Mulrua when they were younger.'

'This raised Liam's suspicions as it questioned the integrity of the kidnapper's note and the fact that it was Mulrua who turned the crooks in. He planned to go to Mulrua to question him and try to get him to confess, which he did. Mulrua killed Mary all those years ago and sent the ransom note to cover his tracks, thinking no one would be able to pay it.' Miguel added.

'But,' Abigail continued. 'When Carl and his friends started robbing and raising the money, he turned them in for fear that he would be exposed. As such Mary was then assumed dead, and the body was never found.'

Rafferty was taking it all in. 'Ok, so Liam Hoban got his confession and then… killed him?'

'He kidnapped Jessica as a bargaining chip. He sent me an email claiming to be Mulrua, and when I arrived, he would give me a choice, either I shoot Mulrua myself and let him go free, or he would kill Jessica,' explained Ryan.

'So why did he kill Mulrua himself?' Rafferty asked.

'Because Mulrua did something rather disgusting. When Liam arrived in Mulrua's office that day he saw the same thing I saw in a photo online. Mary Hoban's body.'

Rafferty looked astounded. 'Excuse me?!'

'That skeleton he used for teaching the human body that was in his office?'

'Jesus Christ!' exclaimed Rafferty. 'He didn't…'

'Keep it as a trophy? Unfortunately, yes, Maybe it was out of guilt, maybe he was just sick. Whichever it was, it caused Liam enough anger to kill right there and then.

I noticed while looking at the online photo. Her body was in the background, and you could see the arm was broken.'

'We'll have to confirm it,' Rafferty mused. 'But that fairly confirms it already.'

'So, he killed Mulrua, hid in a storage room under the office, stayed there until the coast was clear, and planned his next move.'

'He sent us a video call demanding twenty-thousand from Ryan to let Jessica go,' Abigail continued. 'He was going to use the money to escape and create a new identity. He also felt poetic and tried to recreate what his dad felt forty years ago when he received the ransom note.'

'He spent most of his life searching for the answer behind Mary's disappearance.' Ryan admitted sadly. 'Throughout the COVID years, when he was out of school and locked up in his house, he just investigated it so much it consumed him. He got what he wanted, but now it's destroyed him.'

'He wasn't a bad guy or anything,' Jessica muttered. 'He was just consumed with anger and rage. In the end, he let it get the better of him. All he wanted was justice for his aunt.'

'Hopefully, he'll get a good trial,' said Rafferty with hope in his voice. 'Just goes to show people aren't what they seem. The press isn't going to like this news.'

'All this time we thought he was a saint,' Keaton shook his head sadly. 'He played us all for fools.'

'How on earth did he cover it up?' asked Abigail.

'I think there are two ways of looking at it,' Ryan presented. 'A cynical person would say he did it so he wouldn't he suspected. He could have used his family's wealth to cover his tracks and hide any trace of what he had done. He became a local hero to avoid people looking at him suspiciously. Who would look at someone who taught kids for years, did volunteering, charity work, as a murderer?

A cynical would also think like Liam and believe he kept Mary's body a trophy and that he was proud of what he did.'

The others pondered Ryan's thoughts. 'And the other way?' Abigail asked.

'Maybe he became a saint because he felt guilty over what he had done. His anger issues stopped before he went to college, so maybe he recognised he had gone too far and had to sort himself out. Maybe he spent the rest of his life doing everything for his community, trying to redeem himself and forget the demons in his mind eating at him for what he had done.'

'Yeah well, doesn't explain keeping a dead woman's body in his office,' retorted Joel.

'Well,' Ryan continued. 'Maybe he did really love Mary, perhaps he kept the body to remind him of the good times they had together.

So that every time he went to his office or sat down to work, in a way, she was always there with him. And that's what kept him going all these years.'

'Which one do you think kid?' quizzed Keaton.

Ryan had been asking himself that question since Liam was arrested, and kept coming back to the same conclusion. 'Maybe it's better not knowing,' answered Ryan.

'Think of that poor family,' muttered Miguel. 'Carl must have thought Mary died because he failed to raise the money. He's lived with a lie for most of his life.'

'While Mulrua lived a prosperous successful life despite having been a murderer for most of it' gritted Joel angrily. 'Not exactly fair.'

'The family will be informed, and the body will be returned from them.' 'I dare say we owe them a huge apology, Jason,' Keaton reminded.

'It was fortunate that Liam Hoban wasn't the cleverest killer I've ever met. I think there's going to be many more cases like this in the future,' Rafferty sounded concerned. 'Until then though, I want to thank you guys for alerting us to the situation. Truly, we couldn't have done it without you.'

Abigail, Miguel, and Joel all smiled while Ryan gave a small nod.

'Would it be fair to say that we could use a team of young adults ready to tackle crimes similar to this?' Keaton smiled as he asked. 'I think they've shown they can handle themselves.'

'I can put a good word into the Commissioner about it,' assured Rafferty. 'Anyways, I need to go speak to the Hoban household.' Rafferty began to walk to his car, only to remember something. 'One more thing,' he asked turning back to face Ryan and the others. 'Where on earth did you get the money from?'

The others turned and looked at Joel, who was smiling away.

'A friend of mine a few years back got busted for printing fake money. The police destroyed most of it, but I tapped him up this morning and thankfully he had had a little lying around his place. It was nowhere near the amount Hoban was looking for, but we didn't believe he would look past seeing a bag full of notes.

Rafferty looked horrified at Joel's confession but wasn't going to argue any further, he had had a long day and wanted to clear things up with Carl's family before heading home.

'Andrew, I was wondering could you accompany me to the Hoban household to deliver the news?'

'Of course partner, but first I need to speak with my godson,' nodded Keaton.

'That's fair,' nodded Rafferty. 'I'll see you in a few minutes.'

After years apart from each other due to their disagreements after the Striker fire, the two gardaí seemed to have reconciled.

33

'Right, I dunno about you guys but I need a drink,' exclaimed Joel. He turned to Miguel, 'Do they have Guinness in Spain hermano?'

'No, but we are partial to a can or two,' Miguel smiled. 'You guys coming?'

'We'll catch up,' assured Ryan.

Joel and Miguel wandered off leaving Ryan, Abigail, Jessica, and Keaton.

'If all goes well with the Commissioner,' began Keaton. 'We will receive the green light for the founding of the young adult crime team 'Strikerback.''

'That sounds amazing,' beamed Abigail.

'We have all necessary personal, a tech-savvy computer operator, a tough, wisecracking former minor criminal, a bright, mature female harmonizer,'

Keaton paused before looking at Ryan, 'And a former elite police agent leading the team.'

'You want me to lead?' asked a surprised Ryan.

'I think you're the ideal candidate,' replied Keaton.

'So do I,' responded Abigail and Jessica together.

Ryan stood still for a few seconds thinking it over.

'You're not convinced?' guessed Keaton.

'I don't know if I can lead Keaton,' admitted Ryan, he turned to look at Abigail.

'You said it yourself back in the station, for most of my life I've done things solo, I've only looked after myself and I'm not good at leading other people.' He paused and looked at the ground. 'I don't know if I can do it.'

Keaton sighed and smiled.

'I remember the year I first joined the force,' he began. 'I was a mess, I didn't know what I was at, I didn't feel confident chasing criminals, I wanted to quit after a week.' Keaton blinked and laughed a little thinking of his earlier days.

'After a while, I got better, after a year I was helping new guys coming in. The year after I was given the job of District Officer. My superiors said that I had demonstrated great progress and shown a willingness to work on myself and my weaknesses.'

Abigail's eyes widened.

'My point is, sometimes in life we are thrown into situations that we are not fit for, and we have to adapt to overcome and come out stronger. It is out of your comfort zone, but that's a good thing, It forces you to become a better person.'

Ryan was listening attentively.

'Ryan, the fact that you acknowledge you're not a natural leader is a good thing, I've always thought that our greatest strength is knowing our worst weakness, and our worst weakness is not knowing our greatest strength. I see it in you, now you just have to see it yourself.'

Ryan continued to ponder.

'Think about it kid,' assured Keaton. He turned and walked towards Rafferty's car before pausing and turning back like he had forgotten something.

'Listen, Ryan,' Keaton muttered looking slightly uncomfortable. 'I… don't expect you to forgive me for what happened. I don't know if you ever will, but I want you to know that there hasn't been a minute since you walked out…' Keaton was almost choking. 'That I don't regret lying to you.'

'It's ok,' nodded Ryan. 'I forgive you,'

Keaton looked up looking a little surprised.

'I hated you for what you did Keaton,' Ryan continued. 'And I was angry for a long time.' 'But I'm willing to put it behind me now.' 'Life's too short to stay bitter and angry.'

Abigail and Jessica both smiled.

Keaton managed a small smile. 'I hope you don't mind me saying this Ryan, but Richard would've been so proud.'

Ryan nodded once again. 'I'll see you soon Keaton.'

'Take care kid,' Keaton turned and went to join Rafferty, leaving only Ryan, Abigail, and Jessica.

'I think you should do it, Ryan,' pushed Jessica. 'Remember how you used to say how you loved busting criminals a few years ago? Now you've got a team to help you along, a big secret hideout to work from, what more could you want?'

'She's right Ryan, I think the world needs to move on from the COVID years, especially our generation, if we can help even just one more person who hasn't moved forward or has gotten stuck, isn't that the most incredible thing to have the privilege of doing?'

'What about your parents?' Ryan asked. He remembered their conversation by the pool. 'What happened to them being protective?'

'Oh they still are, but I've realised over the past few days that I need to be the one making the calls over what I do in life. They may want what *they* think is best for me, but I need to do what *I* think is best for me. I wanted to do something incredible with my life, and I think this is it.'

Ryan smiled at her. He knew deep down that he needed Abigail if he was going to be anyway successful as a leader.

'You know I've been thinking about what Liam Hoban did over the years, how he spent his life researching into what happened to his parents.'

'He became vengeful and angry.' Ryan began to shiver. 'I don't want that to happen to me.'

'You mean you think you should stop looking?' asked Abigail.

'Not exactly, but if I was to have something else to fight for, something else take my mind off thinking about them, I won't feel the need to go looking as hard.'

Jessica smiled and Abigail ushered him to say it.

'So, your gonna take the job?' she asked with hope in her voice.

'Yes,' Ryan responded emphatically.

The girls beamed at each other.

'Oh and don't worry,' reminded Abigail, 'I'll be right here by your side to remind you when you're being an idiot.'

'And arrogant,' added Jessica.

'And when your plans don't make sense,' winked Abigail.

'And I'll always catch you when you faint after seeing another dead body,' countered Ryan cheekily.

'You do know I could slap you much harder across the face?' warned Abigail.

The two continued to poke fun at each other before heading with Jessica to Keaton's station for a well-earned drink to celebrate.

__Acknowledgements__

The work of a novel is never the work of one person, and there are many people I must thank in this piece. My parents Robbie and Mary are always there to support me every step of the way. My two sisters Sarah and Zoe always provide me humour and inspiration. I was fortunate to work with excellent Fiverr freelancers. A huge thanks must go to worlddesign_06 for the excellent cover choice. My editors lilibokan and familylyfe were on hand to pick up on any errors in the script and also gave excellent insight into how to make the novel more enjoyable. Finally a huge thanks must go to you, the reader for reading *'A Principal Murder.'* Your support is hugely valued by me and the team.

Printed in Great Britain
by Amazon